Lands of our Ancestors
Book Two

Gary Robinson

Dedication

This book is dedicated to Native American
survivors of California's historical holocausts that
devastated Native cultures and communities
and created historical trauma for
generations of California Native Peoples.

Acknowledgments

Many thanks to Cindra Weber of the San
Bernardino City Schools Indian Education Program for her
support of the <u>Lands of our Ancestors</u> series and my other
educational works.

Many thanks also to fourth grade teacher Dessa
Drake of Templeton, California, for her enthusiasm,
feedback and consultation on the book.

The third person to thank is Spanish teacher Paul
Gelles of Midland School for his review and
recommendations for Spanish translations in the book.

Last, but not least, I say a loving thank you to my
significant other, Lola, for all her love, patience and
support over the past fifteen years.

Note to Teachers and Parents

This is the second book of the historical fiction series Lands of our Ancestors. It is the continuing, multi-generational saga of California Natives who experienced several traumatic eras of California history. What happens to the Native California characters in the Lands of our Ancestors series is typical of what may have happened to many California's tribal people during the Mission Period, the Mexican Period, the Gold Rush Era, and the early years of California statehood.

The saga began in Book One with the story of Kilik, Tuhuy and their Chumash family's hardships during the Spanish mission era (1769-1820s).

This second book follows the main characters and their descendants into the Mexican Rancho Period in the 1820s and 1830s.

Watch for the third and final book in the series, which follows this family into the Gold Rush Era, and the early years of California statehood. The characters in Book Two speak Samala Chumash, Spanish and one of the Yokuts Indian languages.

But, so you can understand what the characters are saying, you will read most of their words in English. Occasionally, Spanish words are used and appear in *italics*.

The following is a guide to the Samala Chumash words used as character names in Book One and Book Two, along with their meanings:

Kilik (<u>Kee</u>-leek) - sparrow hawk

Tuhuy (Too-<u>hooy</u>) - rain

Salapay (<u>Sal</u>-uh-pie) - to lift or raise up

Solomol (<u>Soh</u>-loh-mole) - to straighten an
arrow

Wonono (Wo-<u>no</u>-no) - small owl

Yol (rhymes with pole) - bluebird

Stuk (Stuke-rhymes with Luke) - ladybug

Here are a few of the new character names found in Book 2 that come from Samala Chumash and one of the Yokuts tribal languages:

Tah-chi (*Yokuts*) – name of one of the Yokuts
tribes

Lau-lau (*Yokuts*) - butterfly

Toh-yosh (*Yokuts* – pronounced Toe-yosh) – arrow

Supey – (*Samala Chumash* – pronounced Sue-pay) adornment

Taya (*Coastal Chumash* – pronounced Tie-ya) – abalone

Kai-ina (Yokuts) - woman

Alapay (*Samala Chumash* - pronounced Al-uh-pie) - above

Malik (*Samala Chumash* - pronounced Mah-leek) - first born child

Alolkoy (*Samala Chumash* - pronounced Al-ole-koy) - dolphin

Mo-Loke (*Samala Chumash)* – long ago, ancient

The new Samala Chumash words, a few Yokuts words, some Spanish phrases, as well as many English words found in the book, are part of the "Words to Know" section of the Teacher Guide that is available to educators.

The guide contains an overview of the Mexican Rancho Era and many important elements that will help students understand this topic within the context of the California state core educational standards.

Contents

Acknowledgments iv

Note to Parents and Teachers v

Introduction 1

Characters and Relationships 3

Timeline of Events the Series 5

Chapter 1 - Survival Skills 7

Chapter 2 - The Village that Ran Away 21

Chapter 3 - Starting Over 33

Chapter 4 - New Generations 53

Chapter 5 - More of the Same 63

Chapter 6 - Kidnapped 81

Chapter 7 – Vaqueros and Maid Servants 93

Chapter 8 – The Ranchero's Daughter 103

Chapter 9 – The Bear and the Bull 115

Chapter 10 – The Fiesta 127

Chapter 11 – Free at Last 137

Chapter 12 – Ranchero's Revenge 153

Chapter 13 – The Final Showdown 165

Chapter 14 – An Uncertain Future 173

Afterward 179

Bibliography of Research Sources 181

Introduction

This is a work of historical fiction based on historical facts. The characters are made up, but through them you will be able to learn what might have happened to the real Native Americans of California during the end of California's Mission Period and into the Mexican Rancho Period that followed.

You will be able to learn more facts about these periods of history by reading any of the books listed in the bibliography at the back of this book.

As you read this story, ask yourself these questions. What would you do if you had to become a leader of other children who counted on you to protect them from dangerous foreigners? How would you get them to safety and make sure they are fed and cared for?

What qualities and skills would you need in order to do this? How would you react as things got worse as time went by? These are some of the questions that our main characters, Kilik and Tuhuy, and their descendants had to ask themselves as they continued on their quest.

Characters and Relationships in the
Lands of our Ancestors series

Kilik (Miguel) – main character, son of Solomol and Wonono

Tuhuy (Rafael) – Kilik's cousin, son of Salapay and Yol

Stuk (Maria) – Kilik's younger sister

Solomol – Kilik's father

Salapay – Tuhuy's father

Wonono – Kilik's mother

Yol – Tuhuy's mother

Alolkoy – Chumash boy with the children who escaped the mission

Tah-chi – A Yokuts Indian scout for the Place of Condors village

Lau-lau – Kilik's first wife

Kai-ina – Kilik's second wife, mother of Malik

Toh-yosh – Lead warrior for the Place of Condors village

Taya – Tuhuy's wife

Alapay (Andrea) – Tuhuy's daughter and Malik's cousin

Malik (Mateo) – Kilik's son and Andrea's cousin

Mo-Loke – Chumash elder in the Place of Condors village

Diego – Native outlaw and leader of Indians who attacked ranches

Francisco Pacheco – Mexican Ranch owner

Mrs. Pacheco – Ranch owner's wife, mother of Magdalena

Magdalena – Ranch owner's daughter

Esteban - Ranch foreman at Rancho Caballero

Juan - Assistant foreman at Rancho Caballero

Pedro – Head of vaqueros at Rancho Caballero

Timeline of Events in the
Lands of our Ancestors series

1769   First Spanish mission near what is now San Diego

1776   Solomol is born at Place of River Turtles village

1777   Salapay is born at Place of River Turtles village

1792   Kilik is born (when Solomol is 16)

1793   Tuhuy is born

1797   Kilik's sister Stuk is born

1804   Kilik & family go to the new mission

1806   The children escape the mission Summer Solstice

       The children arrive at the Place of Condors village

1811   Kilik marries Lau-lau (Yokuts) - Kilik is 19

1812   Dec. 21 - Earthquake damages missions

       Kilik's unborn baby and wife die same day

1813   Stuk dies from measles brought by visitor

1814   Tuhuy leaves village to live alone

       Kilik leaves the village to exlore

1819   Kilik returns, meets Kai-ina (Yokuts woman)

       Tuhuy returns to village, sees Taya

1820   Tuhuy marries Taya, Tuhuy is 27

       Simultaneous ceremony: Kilik marries Kai-ina

1821   Malik is born to Kilik & Kai-ina

       Mexico wins independence from Spain

1822   Alapay is born to Tuhuy and Taya

1823   Cousins Malik and Alapay begin to grow
        and play together

1824   Kilik begins raiding ranches and missions
        for cattle - age 32

1825   Alapay blends healing and fighting as needed

1832   Kilik turns 40 years old

1833   Tuhuy turns 40 years old

1833   Kilik trains Malik as hunter & warrior
        Alapay learns hunting and fighting skills as well
        Spanish padres expelled from missions
        Mission Indians released
        Francisco Pacheco gets land grant - needs workers
        Epidemic outbreak (flu)

1834-1848 Mexican Rancho Period

1834   Kilik finds crippled father and Aunt Yol
        Pacheco's men raid Condor Village
        Tuhuy and others taken to Ranch
        Tuhuy and everyone held at ranch, must work
        Kilik raids Rancho Caballero, rescues family

Chapter One - Survival Skills

Thirteen-year-old Tuhuy tossed and turned as he tried to sleep on the pile of leaves and branches he was using as a bed. He was dreaming the same thing he'd dreamed for the past few nights. In it, he and several children were trying to find their home village, the Place of River Turtles. It was a place of peace and safety, and he <u>had</u> to get the children there at all costs. Their very survival depended on it.

As the dream continued, he could see the village in the distance, but by the time he reached the spot, the village had mysteriously moved. It reappeared in the distance, and so he headed for it.

Again, it moved to a new spot. And this happened over and over again.

"No, no, no, no!" he cried out in his sleep. "How will we ever find it?"

Then he heard a muffled voice coming from somewhere nearby. It sounded a little like his cousin, Kilik, talking as if he was under water or something. With a jerk, Tuhuy jolted awake.

"What, what?" Tuhuy asked, blinking and looking around.

Tuhuy's fourteen-year-old cousin, Kilik, was kneeling beside him.

"You were screaming in your sleep," he said. "Something about the village moved, and how will we ever find it."

Tuhuy sat up as he realized he'd been dreaming. He told his older cousin about the frustrating dream.

"The elders always said our dreams are trying to tell us something," Tuhuy continued, "But it's up to us to figure out what that is."

Kilik and Tuhuy spoke to each other in their Samala Chumash language, which Kilik's sister, Stuk, understood, as well. A couple of other kids in the group from their home village also spoke the language. But several of the children were from other tribes, brought to the mission from other areas by the Spanish soldiers.

So, in order to understand one another, they had to use hand gestures and a little of the Spanish language, the language of the invaders they'd learned at the mission.

Standing up, Tuhuy saw that all the children were awake and looking at him. He translated the conversation he and Kilik had just had into Spanish so everyone would know what was being discussed.

The group had chosen this hidden spot near a creek to camp for the night. Each child had gathered the brush, leaves and branches needed to make his or her own bed, just as they'd done every night since escaping from the mission. It had been a hard five days since that escape. By day, they had to stay off the main trails for fear of the soldiers.

The children had all seen what the mission priests and soldiers did to captured runaways. At times, Indians who'd escaped were chased by soldiers on horseback, roped like cattle and dragged back. Then they were beaten with a whip, locked in shackles and sometimes starved.

Before their escape, Kilik's father had put his son in charge of the dozen children who made a run for it at dawn on the day of Summer Solstice. Since then, any time Kilik was feeling fearful or uncertain, his father's words came to mind. "Courage comes from within you by joining your mind to your heart. If you love and respect those who need your protection, the courage you need will rise up in spite of any fear you feel."

Those words had proven true, and Kilik had come to trust them during this short, but difficult journey.

"I'm hungry and tired of eating only the seeds, berries and wild lettuce we gather," Kilik's younger sister, Stuk, announced. "When is the great hunter going to bring us some meat, some meat?"

"Ladybug, you shouldn't talk to your brother that way," Tuhuy replied. "He's—"

"No, she's right," Kilik said, interrupting his cousin. "Father put me in charge of protecting our little group and hunting for wild game. I haven't even used the bow and quiver of arrows he gave me."

"No rabbits, though," young Stuk said with a firm tone. "When I was little, my favorite doll was made of rabbit fur--my favorite doll. But I didn't know that a rabbit had to die so I could have a doll."

"All right," Kilik agreed reluctantly. "But they are the easiest to kill, clean and cook."

"I don't care," Stuk said. "I will not eat a bite, no matter how hungry I am. Not a bite!"

"No rabbits, then," Tuhuy said as he looked at his cousin. "Since fox and deer are harder to track and kill, it would be best if I helped Kilik with the hunt."

"But who'll look after us while you're gone?" Stuk asked.

Kilik thought a moment. "Who's the next oldest after me and Tuhuy?"

"I believe Alol-koy is," Tuhuy said after a pause. "Kilik is fourteen. I'm thirteen, and aren't you twelve?" Tuhuy asked Alol-koy, whose name meant Dolphin.

"You two are so good at leading us," Alol-koy replied. "I'm not sure I'd know what to do if something happens," he added.

"If you hear horses coming, find a place to hide," Kilik said. "And if a bear shows up, sit still and sing the Bear Song together. We've sung it every day since we left the mission, so you know it."

"If one of the kids gets scared, tell them a story," Tuhuy added. "And if someone gets a cut, use the medicine herbs we collected near Shrine Mountain. They're in the burlap bag."

"That's what we'd do," Kilik said. "Not that hard."

"You make it sound easy," Alol-koy replied. "I guess I can handle it."

Kilik gathered up his bow and quiver of arrows. He and Tuhuy headed out on their hunt.

The first animal they came across was, of course, a rabbit. Kilik would've loved to bring a couple of them back to camp. But he kept his promise to Stuk, and the boys kept moving.

After a long while of searching in the woods, they found no deer or fox. Circling round through another part of the forest, they crossed the same little creek that flowed by their camp.

"Let's follow this creek for a while, since it will take us back to camp," Kilik suggested. "A deer may come to drink along here."

Moving quietly and trying to keep from stepping on branches or leaves that would make a crunching noise, the boys walked beside the creek. As they made their way around a large boulder at the water's edge, they startled a young deer taking a drink.

The deer looked at the pair for a moment and froze.

Suddenly the animal bolted away at lightning speed, running in the direction of the children's camp.

Kilik and Tuhuy ran after it but couldn't keep up. The deer disappeared among the trees and brush ahead of them.

The boys kept running though, and soon they heard screams coming from the camp.

"The deer must've run into the camp," Kilik said as he ran.

The screaming had startled the deer again, and it reversed direction. It was now headed back toward Kilik and Tuhuy. The boys heard it crashing through the underbrush, so they hid behind a bush and waited. Kilik nocked an arrow, and in a moment the deer came close to them.

Kilik stood up, pulled back the bow and hit the deer just behind the front shoulder.

"I guess all those years of practicing the hoop-and-pole game are paying off," Tuhuy said as they approached the fallen animal. Just as they arrived at the deer's side, it stopped struggling. The boys watched as the deer exhaled its last breath and closed its eyes.

Tuhuy knelt beside the creature, placed his hand over its eyes and offered a prayer to the spirit of the animal. Repeating words he'd learned from his grandfather, a member of the Council of Twelve, the boy thanked the animal for its sacrifice so they could have food.

Kilik was surprised to learn that his cousin remembered just what Samala Chumash words to say at a time like this.

"You still know our Chumash ways after two years at the mission," he said.

"I still remember who I am and where I come from," Tuhuy replied. "Father told me how important it was to never forget that."

"Same with my father," Kilik said. "They are brothers, after all, sons of the same branch of the family tree."

The mention of their fathers reminded the boys of the dangerous conditions they'd left back at the mission. As the children had escaped that sunny morning just a few days ago, a battle raged within those mission walls.

Warriors with mere bows, arrows and lances fought for their freedom against soldiers on horseback who used rifles and steel swords.

The memory was filled with pain and uncertainty. Would they ever see their fathers and mothers again? Would they ever be together as families again? These fears lived in the minds and hearts of all the children that traveled with them

But these two boys, Kilik and Tuhuy, carried a heavier burden on their shoulders. They were responsible for the survival of their little band of children. They were responsible for leading these children to a life of freedom outside the mission walls.

So, without another word, the boys made a quick search of the area and found a sturdy branch and several shoots of the dogbane plant. They fashioned the flexible dogbane stems into lengths of rope just as the Chumash people had done for generations.

Once that was done, the boys tied the deer's legs to the branch. Hoisting the branch to their shoulders, the pair began to march back to camp with the deer carcass swinging between them.

Back in camp, the children were delighted with the thought of deer meat for dinner. But the process of getting from a freshly-killed animal to edible pieces of meat required patience and experience, both of which Kilik had. Tuhuy looked at Alol-koy.

"Why don't you take the children on a search for herbs and berries while Kilik and I prepare the venison?" he asked.

"Good idea," Kilik said as he laid out the carcass on a grassy patch of ground. Alol-koy led the others off into the woods as Tuhuy handed his cousin the flint knife he'd been carrying since they left the mission. The boys went to work skinning the deer and then carving up the meaty portions of the front and hind legs.

As young boys, they'd watched their fathers do this hundreds of times. In recent years before the strangers came, they'd even done the job themselves a few times.

"It's a little risky to build a fire to cook this meat," Kilik told Tuhuy, "but I think we're far enough off the main trail to be safe."

Tuhuy took charge of fire building while his cousin finished butchering the deer. Smoke from the fire drew the children back to camp. The herbs and berries the children had gathered proved useful for flavoring the meat as it cooked over the open flames.

The usually talkative group fell silent as the cooked deer meat was passed around, and they sunk their teeth into the tasty protein. Chewing and swallowing occupied their minds as Grandfather Sun carried his torch beyond the western horizon that evening.

The deer meat not only filled the children's bellies with much-needed solid food but also put everyone in a good mood. As their cooking fire died down and darkness descended on the forest, yawning spread through the group.

"Story time," Tuhuy said, and the young ones made their way to their brushy beds. As their eyes fluttered and closed, he told them how Lizard had tricked Sky-Coyote when humans were being created. People ended up having hands more like Lizard's with four fingers and a thumb instead of Coyote's four-toed paws. Aren't we lucky!

"How much farther do you think it is to the village of runaways?" Tuhuy asked Kilik after the younger ones were asleep.

"Two days, if we pick up the pace," Kilik replied. "I think the deer meat will give us the energy we need to make it by then. Sacred Mountain is not that far away now."

There was no reply from Tuhuy.

"Tuhuy?" Kilik said, but there was still no reply. Kilik realized that his cousin was already fast asleep.

Chapter Two - The Village that Ran Away

Two days later they approached a clearing at the base of Sacred Mountain. Through the trees up ahead, Kilik saw a circle of Tule reed houses. They had arrived!

But the area was mysteriously quiet. They should've heard the voices of people and the sounds of village life. However, there was nothing but silence.

As the group broke through the trees and stepped into the clearing, they found out why. The village was empty, abandoned. The people were gone! But to where?

A couple of the younger children began to cry.

"Now I know the meaning of my dream," Tuhuy said. "It was a warning of this very thing."

Tuhuy tried to comfort the young ones, although he was plenty upset himself.

Kilik looked around the village, poked his head into a couple of the homes and tried to see if there were any clues.

Just then a Native man came down the slope from behind the village and approached Kilik. The man said something in his tribal language, but Kilik didn't understand him.

"Welcome," the man said in Spanish. "I am called Tah-chi, which is actually the name of my Yokuts tribe. In the mission, Indians from other tribes gave me that nickname, and I just kept it. You must be the children that escaped from the mission. Rumors told of your coming."

"Where is everyone?" Tuhuy asked, using Spanish as well.

"We had to move the village," the man replied. "A small group of soldiers found us and began shooting, so we had to fight them off."

"Was anyone killed in the fight?" Kilik asked.

"Unfortunately, several of our people died at the hands of the soldiers," the man replied. "We were forced to defend ourselves, and all the attackers were killed."

Just then two other Indian men came down the slope and into the village.

"These men will stay behind to lead others to the new village site," Tah-chi said. "I will guide you to the new village on the other side of the mountains. It is another two day-journey, but we have food and water for the trip."

"For our people, this mountain is known as Sacred Mountain," Tuhuy said. "Can we take time to climb to the summit so we can offer prayers to our ancestors?"

"It would take most of the day to reach the top," Tah-chi replied. "And then most of a second day to come back down. I think it's best that we move on to the new village in case more soldiers find this place."

"We can come back soon and travel to the top," Kilik suggested. "I want to get the children settled in their new homes first."

Tuhuy saw the wisdom of waiting and was ready to move on. Their guide knew the shortcuts and passes through the mountains that took them to the new village located in the foothills on the far side of the mountain range.

On the second day of the journey they turned a corner in the trail and stepped into a clearing. There, on a flat area of the hillside stood the village. The homes were a mixture of structures. Some looked like the round tule reed huts built by the Chumash in Kilik's home village. Others were cone-shaped buildings made of strips of wood that came together at the top.

Outside the circle of homes there was a ceremonial area, a granary for storing acorns and seeds, and a playing field.

"Tule reeds must grow around here," Tuhuy told Kilik as they gazed at the village. "And these cone-shaped houses are like homes the Yokuts people make. My father described them to me once."

"The name of this village in our language means the Place of Condors, because that sacred bird, the condor, makes its nests in the cliffs nearby," their guide said. "They fly above us almost daily, and so we are blessed."

Below the village, the cousins saw a broad, flat plain unlike anything they'd ever seen in the little valley where the Place of River Turtles was located. Much to Kilik's surprise, plowed rows of bare earth filled parts of the land closest to the base of the hills. And they watched as an Indian man followed behind a horse and plow as new ground was broken up.

"We've blended what we can of Native culture with the skills we learned in the missions," Tah-chi said. "Because we aren't free to hunt game and gather plant foods as much as we traditionally did, we're planting corn, pumpkins and melons down below to feed the growing number of people who escape from the missions."

Then he led the children across to the other side of the village where a wooden corral stood.

Inside the corral was a small herd of horses.

"Where did the tools, crop seeds and horses come from?" Tuhuy asked.

"Where do you think?" Tah-chi answered. "From the missions. I guess you could say we stole them, but the Spaniards have destroyed so much of our traditional lands and ways, we have to find new ways to live and survive."

After the tour, Tah-chi introduced the children to the village elders who stood in a half-circle in the central plaza. They were surrounded by others who lived there.

"Welcome to our humble village," their leader said to them, again speaking Spanish. "We are peoples of different tribes who speak different languages. But we have one thing in common. We have all escaped from the invaders who enslaved us in the missions."

Kilik looked around at the Indian people who had gathered to greet them. They were of every age. Some looked very healthy, while others appeared to be injured or thin and under-fed.

A couple of people had crosses burned into their cheeks, the same way cattle were branded with branding irons.

"Several of our people have volunteered to take you in and make you part of their families, at least for a while," the elder continued.

"Thank you, honored elder," Tuhuy said on behalf of the group of children. "We greatly appreciate your kindness, but we need to find out what's going on with our parents back at the mission."

"We know the fighting has stopped," the elder replied. "But that's all we know for now."

"We are expecting runners to come with more news any day now," a strong-looking younger man said as he stepped forward.

"Excuse me for being impatient, but I'd like to go see for myself as soon as possible," Kilik replied. "My cousin can stay here and make sure our little group gets what they need."

"Wait, what?" Tuhuy blurted out. "I thought we were going to stick together."

The strong man approached Kilik and said, "I am called Toh-yosh in my Yokuts language--Arrow. I lead the warriors in this camp."

"I am Kilik--Sparrow Hawk in my Samala Chumash language," Kilik replied. "And this is my cousin, Tuhuy--Rain. It has been our duty to lead this band of children on our journey to freedom."

"A brave thing you have done," Toh-yosh said to the young cousins. "But these are dangerous times for Indians, and I must insist that you be patient for now. If the time comes for action, then you may join the fight if you feel you must."

Kilik was pleased with the words Toh-yosh spoke. Tuhuy was not.

"What are you doing?" Tuhuy asked his cousin.

"Exactly what I've been training to do," Kilik replied. "Protect our people. That means more than just you and the children. It means everyone who was born in the lands of our ancestors, our native homelands."

That was the moment Tuhuy realized that he and his cousin might <u>not</u> spend the rest of their lives together. They weren't necessarily going to stay on the same path. This thought saddened the boy, but he kept it to himself. He had little to say for the rest of the day as he thought more about their possible separate futures.

All the children settled in with their adoptive families that evening. Though they all missed their parents terribly, each of them was thankful to have people to be with, a place to stay and decent food to eat.

Kilik, Tuhuy and Stuk were all together with a family of Yokuts Indian people. The Yokuts tribal groups were northern neighbors to the Chumash bands. Like the Chumash, the Yokuts had ended up in several different missions scattered along the central California region.

The following day, Toh-yosh knew that Kilik would be restless and anxious to hear news about his parents.

So, he decided to keep the boy busy with lessons on horseback riding. This could prove to be useful to Kilik in the future, especially if he planned on becoming a full-fledged warrior.

This plan worked because Kilik became totally fascinated by the four-legged beasts. Over the next few days, he learned how to care for them, feed them, ride them and even how to shoot at a target with a bow and arrow while the animal was galloping. Hitting that target while riding would, however, take a lot more practice.

A few days had drifted by when two Native riders sped into the village with news about the mission. Jumping off their horses, the pair ran to the elder's house to report. Kilik managed to make his way there in time to hear what the riders had to say.

"The Spaniards have retaken the mission," the first rider said. "And many Native people died during the battle."

"Some of the Native men who took part in the uprising were marched away in chains," the second rider added. "Others were taken to other nearby

---

30

missions to separate them so they cannot plan another uprising."

"Do you have any idea about where the chained prisoners were being taken?" Kilik asked.

The first rider said, "I think they were headed to the military fort, the presidio, in Santa Barbara. Sometimes Indians are taken there to be punished with hard labor."

Kilik did not like the sound of that at all. He left the gathering and went to find his cousin. The boy was in the field down below the village. While Kilik had been learning about horses, Tuhuy had been learning how to plant crops and grow food.

"Are our parents still at the mission?" Tuhuy asked after hearing the news.

"I don't know," Kilik answered. "The riders didn't say."

Toh-yosh, who had also heard the news, came to find Kilik.

"I know you want to ride out and go find your relatives," he said. "But this would be a dangerous and foolish thing to do."

He paused a moment before adding, "You would probably be killed by the soldiers."

"But I can't sit back and do nothing," Kilik complained.

"You won't be doing nothing," the Yokuts warrior replied. "You'll be continuing to train for riding and fighting. Then, when it's the right time, you'll be ready."

Kilik thought about that as Toh-yosh continued.

"The elders have been watching Tuhuy, and they see that he has wisdom beyond his years," he said. "He learns quickly and knows the traditional medicines and the stories of your people. They believe he may develop into a fine healer and spiritual leader."

Tuhuy didn't realize that he'd been noticed by the elders. He was filled with pride. His own path in life was beginning to emerge.

Kilik decided to heed the words of Toh-yosh and patiently wait for an opportunity to ride out in search of his parents.

Chapter Three - Starting Over

As time passed, more Native peoples from different tribes who'd escaped from various missions found their way to the Place of Condors. They brought with them more stories of disease, malnutrition and physical abuse at the hands of their Spanish masters.

Meanwhile, the two cousins matured and got better at the things they loved to do. Kilik went on hunting trips with the men to bring back deer, fox and rabbit meat to the village. He continued to learn and practice the ways of the warrior.

Tuhuy, the quick learner, traveled with the elders into the nearby hills and mountains to look for medicinal plants. He learned how to use more plants to heal people. Sometimes he told the younger children the ancient tribal stories from his ancestors he'd memorized. As newcomers arrived at the village, he would also learn some of their Native language. Those who had escaped from one of the missions taught him new Spanish words and phrases.

Through the years, Kilik and Tuhuy never gave up on finding their parents, who had remained in the mission when the children escaped. From time to time, Kilik left the Place of Condors and rode on horseback to search for them within the five missions built in Chumash territory.

Tuhuy always remained at the village to keep Stuk company.

These trips were dangerous, because Kilik could be caught, captured and taken back to one of the missions. Then, not only would he be back in that hated place, but he'd be separated from what family he had left.

This task of finding their parents was made more difficult because few people outside their own family knew their fathers' and mothers' Indian names.

Like everyone else, they had been given Spanish names, Salvador for Solomol and Santiago for Salapay. But the padres at each mission had given out the <u>same names</u> to dozens of Native people when they were baptized.

There were hundreds of Indians named Salvador, Santiago, Miguel, Rafael, Maria, Jose, Josephina--the list went on and on.

Tuhuy lost track of the number of times his cousin had ridden out in search of their parents. And he also lost track of the number of times his cousin had returned disappointed. As time passed, Kilik rode out less often and decided to focus on the family whose location he knew, the family that represented the future of his own tribe.

Two years had passed since the children had made their escape.

But Kilik still waited impatiently for news to arrive about conditions within the missions or the location of their parents. He questioned every newcomer to the village.

His impatience grew to the point that he decided to try one more time to find out what happened. As a sixteen-year-old, he felt confident that he'd learned enough to take care of himself out on his own.

One morning very early, before anyone else was awake, he grabbed his bow and quiver of arrows. Sneaking quietly through the village, he climbed on his horse and headed out.

After three days of weaving through forests, wading across rivers and riding around mountains, he finally made it to an area he recognized, an area near the mission.

Dismounting his horse, Kilik peered from a hilltop down on the mission he and the children had escaped from. Nothing had changed.

But the boy was unable to see anyone he recognized from that distance.

He had to move closer. He tied his horse up to a nearby tree and began creeping down the hill for a closer look. Halfway down the slope, he heard horses approaching from the west. He quickly jumped behind a clump of bushes to hide.

What came into view was a caravan of soldiers on horseback led by a commandant. In the midst of them, tied by rope and walking on foot, was a line of three Indian men. Their ankles were hobbled with metal chains.

"You will quickly learn what happens to Indians that run away," barked the commandant.

He jerked at the rope that tied all the Indians together. This caused the men to trip on their shackles and fall to the ground.

Then the Commandant gave the order, and the riders began galloping toward the mission.

As the Indians were dragged across the rugged ground, rocks tore at their skin. Kilik was shocked by the sight and gasped aloud.

The soldier at the end of the line heard him and turned to see where the sound had come from.

"Commandant!" the soldier shouted. "Another runaway up on the hill!"

Kilik realized he'd been discovered and had to act fast. He scurried back up the hill and quickly untied his horse. At breakneck speed, he galloped away with two of the soldiers hot on his tail.

Fear pulsed through the Chumash teen's veins as he clung to his horse's mane for dear life. What a terrible idea this had been. What was he thinking?

For a long while, he was unable to shake the soldiers that trailed him. Suddenly Kilik realized that he couldn't ride directly for the Place of Condors. What if the soldiers stayed behind him the whole way? He would be leading the Spaniards straight to his family and friends.

That's when Kilik remembered one of the things Toh-yosh had taught him in his warrior training. The horse soldiers mostly used swords when fighting, but sometimes fired their single-shot pistols.

It was hard to hit a moving target with those pistols, and the weapons took some time to reload.

Kilik, on the other hand, had become quite the expert at hitting a moving target from horseback.

So, this would be it—his first time to confront an enemy. The first question that went through his mind was this.

Did he have the nerve to pull it off? And the second question was: could he actually shoot at another human being? He realized he'd never know until he tried.

He signaled his horse to make an arching turn to the left. He rode back parallel to the soldiers, using the cover of the forest to his advantage. The lead soldier pulled his single-shot pistol and fired at the boy. As the round musket-ball struck a tree beside his head, Kilik let loose an arrow that hit the soldier in the leg.

With a scream of pain, the man yanked on his reins causing his horse to lurch and fall.

One down, one to go.

The second soldier pulled out his own pistol, but realized he couldn't hit his target while on a moving horse.

He yanked the horse to a stop and took careful aim at Kilik. But this action gave the young warrior time to nock a second arrow and bring his own horse to a full stop. Using a tree for cover, Kilik had an easy shot at the man who was sitting perfectly still in the wide open.

This time, the boy's arrow struck the man's left shoulder just as the soldier fired. The man's shot fired harmlessly into the air as he tumbled off the horse and on to the ground.

Now both men lay on the ground moaning in agony. Kilik knew that neither man would die from his wounds. Even though these people had ruined the lives of his family, and he hated them for it, he wasn't quite ready to kill anyone over it.

For now, he had defended himself and stopped the soldiers' attack without taking a man's life. He was pretty proud of himself.

Arriving back at the village, he had quite a wild tale to tell Tuhuy and the others. Toh-yosh first scolded Kilik for going by himself and being so foolish. Then he congratulated the boy on his brave deed. Unfortunately, the cousins were no closer to finding out what happened to their parents.

As more time passed, Kilik and Tuhuy became more interested in the daughters of new families who joined the village. One such girl from a neighboring Yokuts tribe named Lau-lau, or Butterfly, quickly caught Kilik's eye. He sometimes waited for her to take a walk away from her parents, and then he would ride near her, showing off his horseback riding skills.

And, after a hunt, he made a point of bringing some of the choicest cuts of deer or fox meat to her father. Both Lau-lau and her father were impressed by Kilik's skills and thoughtfulness.

At age nineteen, Kilik married Lau-lau, and he built them their own Tule reed house to live in. Like all newly married young people, Kilik often had questions about what's expected in a marriage.

Since Kilik's parents and grandparents were unavailable, he often talked to respected village elders about such matters.

This process wasn't as simple as it could've been since Native people from different tribes had different ways of handling problems at home. But the Chumash boy managed to find out what he needed to know.

The following year, Kilik and Lau-Lau were expecting to have a baby. The village elders watched Lau-lau closely so they'd know about when the baby would be born. They could tell it would be born around the time of Winter Solstice in December.

Meanwhile, Tuhuy met a beautiful girl who came with her Chumash family from a mission located near the ocean. Her name, Supey, meant ornament or adornment. Tuhuy thought this name suited her very well.

Not good at talking to girls, Tuhuy had a harder time letting her know that he liked her. He ended up asking one of the village elders to speak to her and her parents on his behalf.

That's when Tuhuy found out that Supey had already noticed him and liked him especially because he <u>wasn't</u> a showoff like his cousin. The boy was delighted.

He eventually worked up enough courage to ask her to marry him. He decided he'd speak to her and her family about it the following morning. Having tossed and turned most of the night in anticipation, Tuhuy rushed to her home at first light the next morning.

What he found when he got there crushed him. Supey's family home was empty. Her family was gone! He approached the nearest neighbors.

"Do you know what happened to Supey and her family?" he asked anxiously. "Their home is empty."

"A visitor came to see them last night," the neighbor replied. "Supey's family bundled up their belongings and left before daylight."

"But did they tell you why?" Tuhuy asked.

"They said that Supey's brother died of an illness back at the mission they had escaped from," the neighbor answered. "The family wanted to try and get his body back before the padres dumped him in the unmarked mass grave with the others."

"But he will have already been buried before they can get there," Tuhuy protested. "And they'll just be re-captured by the mission."

The neighbor said he told him those very things, but they had made up their minds.

Tuhuy was heart-broken. He knew that going back to the mission was a big mistake, and he knew he'd probably never see Supey again. What would he do now?

Finally, the month of December came, and the time for the birth of Kilik's baby was at hand.

As Winter Solstice approached, the elders watched the night skies as they did every year at that time. The night before the first day of the Winter Solstice, one of the elders saw a disturbing sign in the sky. She told Kilik it meant that trouble was coming. This alarmed the father-to-be, but what could he do?

His wife, Lau-lau, went into labor early the next morning. Two of the elder village women were by her side as she worked to give birth.

Most times Native women had little trouble bringing a baby into the world. But this day was different. Lau-lau pushed and pushed, but the baby inside her belly wouldn't budge.

Later in the morning, when Grandfather Sun was still low in the sky, the ground beneath them began to shake.

And it continued to shake. Lau-lau looked to the elder women for an answer. What was happening?

Suddenly the mother-to-be screamed out it pain and grabbed her belly. It felt like someone was stabbing her with a knife. Kilik held his wife and tried to calm her.

People in the village were fearful, as well, for they believed that powerful dark forces within the earth caused the shaking. They thought that humans must've done something to anger these supernatural forces.

In the midst of the worst shaking, Kilik suddenly felt Lau-lau's life-force drain from her. Her body became limp.

He, too, looked to the elder women for answers. They listened intently for signs of life in Lau-lau's body but could find none.

They put their ears to the woman's belly and listened for signs of life within her baby. They could find none there either.

"They are gone, my son," the eldest woman said in a kind voice. "Mother Earth is not pleased with what's been happening in the lands of our ancestors since the strangers came among us. Things are out of balance, and she is resetting that balance."

What neither Kilik or the elders knew was that this earthquake of December 21, 1812, had shaken the lands far and wide.

Several of the missions in the region had been shaken furiously. Their buildings crumbled, and lives were lost. Tragedy visited Spaniard and Indian alike.

And that wasn't to be the end of the tragedies in Kilik's life.

The following year, a Native teenager who had escaped from the mission found his way to the village. The handsome young man was ill and said that many Indians in the mission had died of a strange sickness.

The family that Kilik's sister, Stuk, lived with volunteered to take the boy in and care for him. Obtaining herbal remedies from Tuhuy, the sixteen-year-old Stuk gave him regular treatments. But Indian medicines didn't seem to help. To make matters worse, Stuk became sick as well.

Within a week, both the boy and Stuk died of the illness. Traditional Native treatments were no match for this European disease known as measles.

Within a short period of time, Kilik and Tuhuy had both suffered losses.

Each had his own way of dealing with those losses, but they had one thing in common: the need for solitude.

Tuhuy, the thinker, gathered up a few of his belongings, some dried deer jerky and other portable foods. He felt the call of wilderness and decided to answer that call. Alone. Bidding his cousin farewell, he headed first for Sacred Mountain. He would finally make that journey to the top to speak to his ancestors.

Kilik, the doer, then gathered up his bow and quiver of arrows and climbed on his horse. He felt it was time to once again search for his and Tuhuy's parents who were still somewhere within the mission system. He needed to be busy doing something to keep his mind off his own dire loss, and this was the only thing he could think of.

As time continued to pass, life became more difficult for the people of the Place of Condors, and for all California Indians. Drought was killing plants and animals, and there seemed to be no end of settlers moving closer to them and gobbling up land and resources.

On his journey, Tuhuy decided to refresh his knowledge of plants and their traditional uses. He had learned much from his own grandfather back in their home village, the Place of River Turtles. This knowledge had been passed down through countless generations of Chumash healers.

But as time passed, he felt a prompting to go inward within his own soul.

Exploring the depths and heights of this inner world, he unexpectedly found a way to communicate in spirit with his Chumash ancestors.

Not many people could do this. Among other things, the ancestors taught him a new way to heal both Natives and non-Natives. He believed this would help him and his descendants to survive one day.

On his very different journey, Kilik explored physical territories as far as the eye could see. Careful to stay out of the sight of the foreign settlers, he traveled the countryside and observed their ways of doing things. He believed this would help him and his descendants to survive one day.

Kilik joined a band of roving Indians that had all lost someone to the missions or to the diseases brought by the foreigners. To survive, they raided Spanish settlements to steal horses or cattle to feed themselves and other outcast Native peoples.

Angry at the destruction of his family and his Native lands, Kilik poured all his energy into disrupting the colonists' lives.

On one of the early raids, he noticed a sparrow hawk, his name sake, flying above him as he and his horse rested near a stream. The bird dropped one of its feathers. It drifted down and landed nearby. He took it as a blessing from the ancestors.

That's when the idea struck him. He would gather falcon and hawk feathers wherever he went and carry them with him. Then, when he raided a mission, ranch or settlement, he would leave one behind as kind of a signature, telling the foreigners who had raided them.

The young Chumash man honed his fighting and raiding skills until he became the leader of his pack of Indians. And, as the number of feathers he left behind grew, so did his notoriety.

No one knew what to make of this mysterious Indian who stole livestock and left a hawk feather.

Some Spaniards thought he must be a ghost, because no one ever saw him come and go. Others considered him a demon who struck in the middle of the night without warning and then disappeared.

But, because of the feathers, both Spaniards and Natives came to know him by a new nickname: The Falcon.

The Falcon operated for years using his hit-and-run technique. And other Indians began using the same tactic for raiding ranches and stealing cattle. As often happens with legendary outlaws, many raids conducted by others were attributed to The Falcon. He was often reported to be in two very distant locations at the same time! Such is the stuff of legends.

But, even though Kilik and Tuhuy were separated by miles and by different kinds of experiences, the cousins seemed to maintain a link between them. They were connected more like twins than cousins. And not surprisingly, each felt the urge to return to the Place of Condors at about the same time.

Time for new beginnings. Time to start over.

Chapter 4 - New Generations

The two boys originally from the Place of River Turtles reunited after their long years of separation. However, they were no longer boys. Kilik was now twenty-seven years old, and Tuhuy twenty-six. Tuhuy knew nothing of his cousin's additional identity, the Falcon, or of his life as a famous Native American outlaw. Kilik wanted to keep it that way for the time being.

The year was 1819, and what Kilik, Tuhuy and what the people of the Place of Condors didn't know was that the lands of their ancestors had been claimed as part of a vast empire called New Spain.

Thousands of colonists from Spain had been settling in these territories since the first mission was built in 1769. Part of these territories further south included an area called Mexico, and the colonial rulers of California lived in that country.

But, in the years leading up to the 1820s, the citizens of Mexico wanted to be independent of Spain and have their own government. Battles were being fought hundreds of miles away between the citizens of these two nations. Whoever won that war would rule over the lands of California's Native peoples.

In 1821, the Mexicans won their independence.

That meant that Alta California became a territory of Mexico with a new government, new rulers and new rules.

At first, these events didn't really make any difference in the lives of Indians who lived in a remote village. As the years of the 1820s passed, however, changes would take place that impacted the lives of Natives, and not for the better.

A new set of Indian people had moved to the Place of Condors while the two cousins were away. This included a new set of young Indian women. A woman from one of the Yokuts tribes named Kai-ina caught Kilik's eye. A little older and wiser now, he no longer felt the need to show off for her.

Tuhuy had gotten over his shyness with the opposite sex and developed a fondness for a Chumash woman a few years younger than himself.

Her name was Taya, meaning Abalone, a small sea creature that lived in a very colorful shell.

Continuing in their connected lives, the Chumash cousins got married on the same day in a shared ceremony. Everyone in the village celebrated these weddings. These events brought hope that their futures would be better than their pasts.

A year later both couples shared in the joys of childbirth. A son was born to Kilik and Kai-ina, and they named him Malik, a Samala word meaning "First-Born Child." Kilik felt this was a good name because his first child died without ever being born.

Tuhuy and Taya's child, born three months later, was a girl. Before she was born, Tuhuy had dreamed about the girl.

In the dream, he was walking beside a gently flowing stream in the woods.

He stooped down and scooped up a handful of the clear water. As he sipped the water, a bear cub walked right up to him and calmly said, "I am coming to be with you soon, Koko." Koko is the Samala word for father. When Tuhuy awoke from the dream, he knew he soon would have a beautiful daughter, but he wasn't sure what the bear meant.

He found out the day she was born, because she had a birthmark on her cheek that looked like a bear claw. This was a sign that she would do great things. They named her Alapay, meaning Above, because that name reminded them of Tuhuy's father's name, Salapay.

Toh-yosh, the warrior, came to both families not long after their children were born to offer them some advice about their children's names.

"Spanish-speaking people are spreading across the lands of our ancestors like a flood," he said. "They're building towns and ranches from mountain to mountain and from the ocean to the inland rivers."

Though neither of the boys had ever thought about this, they knew that the warrior's words were true.

"I hate to say it," he continued. "But, in addition to the traditional tribal names you give your children, you should think about giving them Spanish names as well."

"Why would you say such a thing?" a shocked Kilik asked. "We are pledged to keep our tribal traditions alive in the face of this great invasion of strangers."

"It is only because I am thinking of your children's very survival in the years to come," Toh-yosh replied. "An elder from my home village saw the future years ago, a future where we are strangers in our own lands. We Indians will have no place in that future unless we <u>outwardly</u> dress like them and behave like the invaders. In our hearts, we will remain who we are. But to survive this flood of outsiders, we must blend in with them."

This hit the new fathers very hard. Kilik and Tuhuy had experienced first-hand the actions of the Turtle-men, the soldiers, and Coyote-men, the priests. The two cousins hated everything about the foreigners who had ruined their lives. Yet soon they might have to pretend to be part of them? The idea didn't feel good at all.

"My Spanish name is Ignacio, given to me by the mission padres," Toh-yosh said. "As I fight for my freedom and the freedom of Native people, I will be known by that name out in the world. Here at home I will remain Toh-yosh--Arrow."

"The padres gave me the name Rafael," Tuhuy said. "Kilik was called Miguel, and Stuk was named Maria, but we never used those names."

"There's another reason for giving your children Spanish names," Toh-yosh advised.

"There are people among the invaders who are known to be witches," he continued. "These dark people can use your true name, your Indian name, against you in black magic ceremonies. If they never learn your Indian name, then you'll be safe from this danger."

After Toh-yosh left them, the cousins talked about these things a long time.

Reluctantly, Kilik gave Malik the Spanish name Mateo, and Tuhuy decided on the name Andrea for Alapay.

"I hope these children never have to use those names," Kilik said.

Malik and Alapay grew into strong young people who were adapting to the changing, dangerous and unpredictable times they lived in. Like their fathers before them, these two young cousins became closely bonded in mind and heart. Their strong connection was destined to serve them well in the years ahead.

As Malik grew, Kilik and Kai-ina tried to teach him as much about the Native ways as they could. But the young parents also taught the boy the realities of this new world.

Tuhuy and Taya tried to teach Alapay how to gather and use natural plants and herbs as their ancestors had done. But the plants were disappearing. The parents also tried to show their daughter how to plant the seeds and grow the foods that had come from the missions. The continuing drought also made this hard.

But as the girl grew, she showed signs of being as much like her uncle as her father. She was drawn to the spear, the bow and the horse as well as the plants and herbs. Tuhuy wasn't particularly pleased with this development, but he believed he had to let his daughter become who she was to become.

So, Kilik took on the task of teaching both his son and his niece the techniques of hunting and fighting. Teaching them to hunt was hard because wild animals were disappearing from the wilderness.

Of course, there was always the hoop-and-pole game for target practice.

But the only time there was enough meat to eat was when Kilik or one of the other village men ventured onto mission or ranch lands to steal cattle. Kilik, the Falcon, knew a person could get killed or captured doing that, so he was very cautious.

Also, during these years, Kilik spent much of his time patrolling the lands around the Place of Condors and beyond as one of the warriors dedicated to protecting the people. Men in these patrols kept a watchful eye out for anyone who didn't belong in the area.

A lone, non-Indian rider just passing through the area might stumble on the village, and then report that information back to Mexican colonial leaders.

In such cases, Kilik and the others chased strangers away before they could discover that a village full of Indians rested just beyond the hill. Malik and Alapay learned these skills, as well.

Like the generation before them, cousins Malik and Alapay were best of friends. Neither one could imagine what life would be like without the other.

So, two generations of this Native family persevered together, happy to have one another for support and survival in those tumultuous times.

But all that was about to change. The most serious threat to the Native villagers was the possibility of an expedition of soldiers who'd been sent into the wilderness specifically to search for Indians that could become laborers for California colonists.

Chapter 5 - More of the Same

Three big events took place in the year 1833 that would once again change the lives of Kilik, Tuhuy and their families forever. First, a deadly flu epidemic spread like wildfire through California Indian communities, killing thousands of people.

When the disease reached Tuhuy's village, people complained of sweating, fever, chills, and dizziness, as well as head and stomach pains. Within a few days, many people had fallen victim to the disease.

Father and daughter healers Tuhuy and Alapay quickly went into action, using what Tuhuy had learned from his ancestors. They identified additional medicinal plants they hoped would cure this strange illness. Fortunately, these worked to heal the people of the Place of Condors.

"Why wouldn't our ancient traditional medicines work on this ailment?" Alapay asked her father.

"I believe it is because the white men brought this sickness with them," Tuhuy replied. "Our ancient treatments work on diseases from this land, not on those from foreign lands. The intruders' bullets are more powerful than our simple arrows, and likewise, their illnesses are more powerful than our ancient Indian medicines."

The second big event taking place that year was the closing of the missions.

The Mexican government expelled the Spanish Franciscan priests from those institutions and took over all the mission lands. Those lands were supposed to be given to mission Indians for them to live on so they could grow crops and raise animals for food and income. For most Natives, that didn't happen.

In a few rare cases, a few Indians received a little bit of land and a few head of cattle they were to use to support themselves. But, in traditional Native American cultures, there was no such thing as land ownership. The Creator gave human beings land, air and water for <u>everyone</u> to use and live on. Nobody could own the land. That was a foreign idea.

Europeans had created a way to divide up the land and become owners of pieces of it. They brought that concept with them to the Americas.

And so, thousands of former mission Indians found themselves with no place to live or work and no way to obtain food.

The third big thing that happened that year involved a large piece land from one of the missions. The Mexican citizens living in Alta California became known as Californios.

One such Californio named Francisco Pacheco received a 33,000-acre land grant from the

Mexican government in an area not too many miles from the Place of Condors. Pacheco's land grant was but one of hundreds given to Californios that year and in the years to follow.

Pacheco named his land *Rancho Caballero*, Gentleman's Ranch.

He planned to raise cattle on the land—cattle that would grow, mature and, one day, be slaughtered for meat to eat and hides to sell.

He knew that kind of large-scale operation would, of course, require a large labor force. And he knew exactly who would make up that labor force: the Indians of California, just as they had done in the missions.

A group of Pacheco's men, accompanied by a group of Mexican soldiers, found their first Indian laborers at one of the abandoned missions near the ranch. These Native men, women and children were practically starving. Pacheco promised them food, a place to stay and small payment if they came to his *rancho* to work. They all readily agreed.

What else could they do? Their villages had been destroyed, their traditional life-ways lost.

The plants and animals that they relied on were disappearing at an alarming rate. But once the former mission Indians moved to the ranch, they were in for a rude awakening.

Sure, they would receive daily rations of barely edible food along with an uncomfortable place to sleep. But there was to be no pay.

Discovering this harsh reality, several Natives tried to leave. However, they found horse-mounted ranch hands, *vaqueros*, and soldiers blocking their way.

So, life on the ranch proved to be a lot like life in the mission—more of the same.

When the people of the Place of Condors heard that the Indians in the missions had been released, they were overjoyed.

Maybe that meant they would no longer have to hide out. Maybe that meant they could be reunited with long-lost relatives.

To Kilik, that meant that he might be more successful in finding his and Tuhuy's parents!

"I will ride to the mission one more time to see if our parents have returned there," he announced to the family.

"And I will go with you," Malik announced to his father.

"Not yet," Kilik said. "There may be soldiers or ranch owners out there, and who knows what they might do to Indians they find. It still may not be safe."

"But-"

"But nothing," Malik's mother said before he could say another word. "We need you here to help with the chores," she continued. "And you can ride on patrol outside the village with the men."

"What about me?" Alapay added. "You know I've been training right alongside Malik. I can patrol and defend the village as good as he can."

"Ha!" Malik protested. "You couldn't-" Once again Malik was interrupted, this time by Alapay's mother, Taya.

"That's enough," she said. "We know both of you are capable of riding horses and shooting arrows. No need to squabble. In one or two years, Alapay, you'll be going with your uncle on one of his distant journeys. There'll be plenty of time for such things."

"That settles it then," Kilik told them. "Malik and Alapay will stay here to help with chores and patrol the woods, if their mothers approve."

"Ahhh," Malik and Alapay responded in unison.

So Kilik, now a forty-one-year old man, set out on horseback once again hoping to find their aging parents, Solomol, Wonono, Salapay and Yol. With a rope, Kilik pulled a second horse behind him just in case he found a relative who needed a ride back to the Place of Condors.

As he rode, the Chumash man thought of the many wonderful times he had as a child back in his home village. He remembered countless things he'd learned from his father and the experiences they had together. Solomol was a skilled hunter and craftsman. Kilik happily pictured the day his parents would finally get to meet their grandson, their Unu.

Kilik headed for the mission that he and the children had escaped from. He hoped that Indians who'd been transferred to other places might have returned to their "home" missions.

It was mid-day as he approached the mission compound. He was surprised to find the place falling apart. With no one to make and replace adobe bricks, the walls were crumbling. With the mission lands in the hands of ranch owners, there was no way to grow food crops.

Kilik stepped down from his horse and tied both animals to a fence rail. Walking along the archway of the main building, he saw a few elderly Indians that still lived on the grounds. These people, all former slaves, seemed to be mostly crippled or malnourished or both.

An older man approached. He walked with a cane and looked like he was in his sixties. There was something vaguely familiar about him, Kilik thought.

"Kilik, is that you?" the man said with a surprised look on his face. "Son?"

Kilik could barely believe his eyes.

"Father?"

He ran to the man he'd been searching for all these years, took him by the shoulders and looked into his eyes.

"Father, it _is_ you!" the younger man said with excitement.

He embraced Solomol with a hug that nearly knocked the older man over. "I thought I'd never see you again."

A tear formed in the corner of Kilik's father's eye.

"And for all these years," Solomol said. "I never knew for sure if you survived after leaving the mission."

The two embraced again in a tearful reunion.

"Your Aunt Yol is here, too," Solomol said after the hug. "She's in the kitchen cooking up the last of the food we have."

Kilik looked his father up and down, noticing his crippled leg.

"What happened to you?" the younger man asked. "Why do you limp and walk with a cane? And where is my mother?"

"Those are sad stories," Solomol replied with a frown. "What I've got now are mostly sad stories. Much has happened since you left the mission on that Summer Solstice day."

The older man began to sway a little. He put his hand to his forehead.

"I'm getting a dizzy spell," he said. Let's go sit down out of the sun, and I'll tell you about it."

And so Kilik heard the sad stories Solomol had to tell. After the children escaped all those years ago, the fighting between Indians and soldiers at the mission continued for another week. Then Spanish reinforcements arrived, allowing the soldiers to retake control. That's when the punishments began. Some were whipped. Some were chained up. Others were marched on foot to the nearest presidio.

The head of the mission guard, El Capitan Castigar, chained Kilik's father to a tree in the central plaza. Then the captain brought Solomol's wife, Wonono, before the chained Indian. Her cheek was swollen where she'd been hit.

Next, the captain commanded one of the soldiers to strike Kilik's father hard in the leg with his rifle. The man whacked it as hard as he could.

Solomol cried out in pain. Finally, Castigar climbed up on his horse and pulled Kilik's mother up on the horse's saddle with him. She screamed and fought to escape, but couldn't.

"I am taking your wife with me," Castigar told Solomol. "She will become my personal servant, and you will never see her again!"

With that, he rode away, taking Wonono with him. Solomol never saw her or Castigar again.

This news hit Kilik hard. Tears began to well up in the corners of his eyes. He wiped them away quickly as he tried to push aside this deep feeling of loss and disappointment. But more tears fell in their place.

He'd held back his grief all these years, foolishly allowing himself to hope he would see both his parents again, alive and well. Then things would go back to being the way they were before the strangers had shown up.

Now, seeing his crippled father and hearing of the kidnapping of his mother, those hopes were dashed. Grief flooded in like heavy rain falling and rushing down a steep mountain slope.

"I knew they were cruel men," Kilik managed to say as he choked back further feelings of sadness. "But I didn't think they were that bad. What about Uncle Salapay?"

"He was taken by soldiers to the presidio just over the mountain where he was to stay for ten years doing hard labor," Solomol said. "But he died there. No one knows how or why. Rumors say one of the white man's diseases killed him. Others say he was killed while trying to escape. I guess we'll never know for sure."

This was another blow to Kilik's all-ready hurting heart.

"As for me, without a doctor's treatment, my leg bone didn't heal properly," he said, finishing up his sad stories. "So, I've hobbled around ever since. They sent me down the road to the next nearest mission along with your Aunt Yol. She and I have tried to take care of each other ever since, and we came back here hoping you'd find us one day."

"Well, now you have your son and grandson to take care of you," Kilik said to cheer himself and his father up.

"What!?" Solomol said excitedly. "I have a grandson!?"

"And a grandniece," Kilik added. "I'll tell you all about them on our ride back to the village."

After eating the plate of food his aunt had prepared, Kilik put his father and Yol on the extra horse. Off they rode toward the Place of Condors. On the trip, Kilik also had to share his own sad stories: the loss of his first wife and unborn child; the death of his sister, Stuk; the disappearance of Tuhuy's girlfriend and family.

Solomol was crushed to learn of the death of his daughter, Stuk. The father had also not allowed himself to fall into despair all these years in the hope of reuniting with his children.

His joy of seeing his son and also learning of his daughter's death was the very definition of the word bittersweet.

As their journey continued, both men wished for happier times, but this was not to be.

Late in the afternoon on the third day of their ride back to the village, Kilik, Solomol and Yol came into the clearing that was the site of the Place of Condors. Their already sad eyes beheld yet another tragedy. Most of the Tule reed homes were nothing but smoldering black ash. The horse corral was empty, and the field crops down the hill had been torched.

Kilik dismounted his horse and ran to the pile of ashes that had been his house. Then he ran to the area where Alapay's family home once stood. No trace of either family could be found.

"It's the same as the missions all over again," Solomol commented as he got off his horse. "They burned our villages so we'd have no place to return to."

"It was a terrible thing to witness," a voice behind them said. They turned to see a withered old Indian man named Mo-loke coming toward them.

"Who did this?" Kilik asked him.

"Vaqueros and soldiers on horseback," Mo-loke replied as he continued toward them. "They surrounded the village at dawn. Each of them held a burning torch. Their captain announced that they were here to round up the thieves who'd stolen the horses from his ranch. He called it *Rancho Caballero*. I told him no one here did that, but he just spit on me."

"Was anyone from the village hurt?" Solomol asked.

"The warrior, Toh-yosh, shot an arrow at their captain," the elder said. "It hit the man in the leg, but, sadly, another soldier fired his pistol. Toh-yosh fell to the ground dead."

Kilik could hardly believe what he was hearing. Toh-yosh had been a substitute for his own father since coming to this village.

"The young ones, Malik and Alapay, wanted to get their weapons and fight," Mo-loke continued. "But their mothers wisely stopped them."

Kilik's Aunt Yol spoke up.

"What about my son, Tuhuy?" she asked.

"He advised everyone in the village to remain calm and follow their orders," the old man replied. "These men were cruel and cared nothing about the welfare of our people. So, I think Tuhuy's words prevented anyone else from being killed."

"Which direction did they go?" Kilik asked.

"The *vaqueros* rounded up our people like cattle and herded them off towards the northwest. They left a few of us old people behind."

"I must go after them and free them," Kilik declared.

"You are but one man," Solomol said. "What can one man do?"

"Well, this one man can't stay here and do nothing," Kilik replied as he climbed up on his horse. "I will follow their trail so I can find where this *Rancho Caballero* is located. I'll decide what to do after that. I'm sorry, but I must leave you once again, father."

"Come back to me soon, my son," Solomol called out. "And bring my grandson with you!"

With strong determination, Kilik set out on his quest, leaving his father with the other elders at the Place of Condors.

Chapter 6 - Kidnapped

As they were marched from their burning homes, the people of the Place of Condors feared for their lives. Many cried aloud, while others simply whimpered. With swords drawn, the soldiers were ready to cut any villager that gave them trouble. The *vaqueros* rode with lassos at the ready to capture anyone attempting to flee.

Tuhuy had, for most of his life, looked to Kilik when it came time for bravery or for figuring out what needed to be done at times like these.

But Kilik was not there. Tuhuy now had only himself to rely on. He would have to call on his own experiences, his own skills and his own courage.

"Stay as close together as you can," he advised the members of his family as they stumbled over the miles of uneven ground. "Give these men no reason to thrust their swords into our bodies or throw their lassos around our necks."

Traveling in a north, and then westerly, direction, the group skirted the mountain range that separated interior California from coastal California. The going was rough, and little food or water was offered to the captives.

Malik and Alapay stayed particularly close to one another on the trek. In whispered tones spoken to one another in the Samala Chumash language, the two vowed to do something to escape. Unknowingly, they made the same vow that Solomol and Salapay had made a generation earlier. Somehow, some way, some day, they would escape from these foreign intruders.

Tuhuy noticed a soldier watching the whispering youth and he shushed them before they could be punished.

After two dry, dusty days of walking, the people of the Place of Condors arrived at the ranch. The thirty-three-thousand-acre property stretched across a vast valley floor.

Running through the middle of the space was a wide riverbed.

However, only a trickle of water ran through it. Two mountain ranges, to the north and south of the land, formed part of the ranch's borders.

There to greet the Natives at the entrance to *Rancho Caballero* was Francisco Pacheco himself, sitting on a beautiful black stallion. The large, overweight *ranchero* had dark, thick sideburns and a bushy black mustache. On his head sat a large-brimmed hat.

"Welcome to your new home," he said with a broad smile. "I hope you will be happy here working for me." Then his smile transformed into a scowl.

"Actually, I don't care if you're happy or not. One way or the other, you will be working for me."

Then, addressing the soldiers, he ordered, "Take them to the workers' dormitories!"

As the soldiers marched the captives away, Pacheco added one more piece of advice.

"Those who try to escape will wish they were never born," he said and laughed loudly and fully.

There's an evil man, Malik and Alapay simultaneously thought to themselves.

To Tuhuy, the ranch was an eerily familiar scene. On the grounds, he saw partially completed buildings made of adobe bricks. Other Indians were laboring to make more bricks and place them one atop the other to create walls. A similar scene had greeted him on the first day he laid eyes on the mission when he was a boy of eleven years.

This time, rather than separate the Natives into men's, women's and family dorms, everyone was led into a large, half-finished adobe space.

The building had a dirt floor, and its ceiling was made of Tule reeds spread across wooden beams.

Waiting for them inside the vacant room was a Mexican foreman who smoked a cigar and held a whip. Tufts of curly black chest hairs peeked out through the open front of his sweat-stained white shirt. Wide suspenders held up his very worn and dirty pants.

"My name is Esteban," he said in a loud voice. "You'll sleep here for the time being. Tomorrow we'll see who can do what. If you have any useful skills or work experience, which I doubt, you won't have to work in the fields."

Leaving several armed ranch-hands guarding the doors, the foreman stomped away chewing on his cigar.

"One of us has to sneak out of here immediately and find my father," Malik whispered to Alapay and Tuhuy, who stood nearby. "He can figure out a way to free us."

"Don't do anything foolish," Alapay cautioned. "I think we need to wait and watch for the right time to slip away."

"Neither one of you is going to do anything," Tuhuy said sternly. "It's too dangerous. Just follow orders and don't cause trouble. And now is the time to put your knowledge of the Spanish language to use, along with those Spanish names we never used. From now on you will be called Mateo and Andrea. I am Rafael."

The harsh new realities of ranch life began the very next day. Esteban made it clear that, in exchange for their labor, the Indians would be paid only in food, clothing and a place to sleep. Then the foreman and a couple of his men had all the Natives line up so they could find out if anyone had any useful skills.

Tuhuy made sure the men spoke to him before approaching the rest of his family group.

"I am known as Rafael, and you'll find that I speak three languages," he told Esteban in his best Spanish. "Samala Chumash, a little of the Yokuts Indian language, as well as some Spanish. I know how to plant and grow crops and treat sick people with herbal remedies. I think I'd be useful as a supervisor of your Indian laborers."

This impressed the foreman, but he tested Tuhuy's knowledge by asking him a few questions on these subjects. When Esteban was satisfied that the Indian knew what he was talking about, he pulled Tuhuy out of the line.

"Juan, come here," the foreman called across the room in a loud voice. "I want you to take this man and show him our entire ranch operation. I think he's going to become our new *Jefecito Indio*!"

Esteban's men all laughed heartily at what seemed to them to be a joke.

"No, I'm serious," Esteban said. "This man seems to think he can help us make these Indians behave, so I want to see how he does."

Tuhuy was trying to make the best of a bad situation. By being put in an important position on the ranch, he hoped to improve the treatment of the Native workers, especially his own family. This was a risky move, but he thought he could pull it off.

"I can save you some time because I already know what skills the people of my village have," Tuhuy added. "For example, my nephew, Mateo, is young, but he is already good on horseback. He could train to become a *vaquero*."

"You are pretty smart for an Indian," Esteban said. "What did you say your name is?"

"Rafael," the Chumash man replied. "A mission padre told me it means God Heals."

Just then, Esteban's assistant, Juan, arrived at the foreman's side.

"This one is called Rafael," Esteban told Juan. "I am putting him in charge of supervising the new Indian workers."

"But boss, he's just an ignorant Indian," Juan protested. "Our own men can handle these peasants much better."

Esteban slapped the Mexican man hard in the face.

"That will be enough out of you!" Esteban snapped. "If you ever question my orders in front of the workers again, I'll cut your tongue out!"

"Yes, boss. Sorry, boss," the man said, bowing his head.

"First, you will show him how everything works here at the ranch so he knows what jobs we have," the foreman ordered.

"Then you will come back here and listen to what he says about who among his people can do what job," he added.

"Yes, boss," Juan replied. "Right away, boss."

In a firm voice the foreman then told Tuhuy, "I'm going to try you out as the new *Jefecito Indio*, but if you fail me, I'll send you to the stables to shovel horse dung all day long!"

Tuhuy knew the man was serious, and he just nodded as Esteban marched away. So, Juan began the tour of the ranch. He started with the main house, a two-story structure that was only about half built. When finished, it would be a square adobe with a central courtyard. Right now, the building was in a U-shape, missing the last portion that would complete the square.

"Señor Pacheco and his family live in the rooms upstairs," the foreman's assistant said.

"Several Indians serve there and cook the family's meals, wash their clothes, clean their rooms--all the domestic duties. I think there is a need for one or two more servants up there now, but it requires the best behavior and polite manners."

Tuhuy thought how perfect it would be for his own wife and daughter to be placed there. They would probably be treated well in the main house and be out of harm's way.

"Downstairs is where things like saddles, boots, rugs, blankets and candles are made," Juan continued. "Most of these Indian craftsmen came from the missions where they learned those skills."

As the two men walked through the space, Tuhuy saw Natives working hard at their jobs under the watchful eyes of whip-toting ranch supervisors.

The Indians appeared underfed, poorly dressed and exhausted. Ranchero Pacheco's words rang in Tuhuy's ears: "I don't care if you're happy or not. One way or the other, you will be working for me."

At one corner of the main house was a set of

stairs the led to the second floor. Tuhuy followed Juan up those stairs where he found a covered walkway that gave you access to all the upstairs rooms. Stopping at a corner post of that walkway, Juan pointed toward a nearby stable and corral.

"Our horses are cared for, fed and trained over there," he said. "Hundreds of horses are needed for herding the thousand head of cattle Señor Pacheco owns."

Tuhuy watched as a Mexican ranch hand threw a saddle up on the back of a beautiful black stallion.

"The *vaqueros* are preparing Señor Pacheco's horse," Juan explained. "Today he will be inspecting the fields at the northern edge of the ranch to see how the crops are growing."

Juan led Tuhuy along the walkway to the far corner of the building and pointed to a pasture filled with cattle. A cowboy was roping a steer as two Indians with knives stood by.

"*Rancho Caballero* will be celebrating its first year of operation soon, and there is much to be done to prepare," Juan said. "They'll be butchering several head of cattle so we'll have meat to serve to our many guests."

Juan turned and headed back down the stairs, talking as he walked. "So, you and your Indians will have a lot of work to do to get ready. Everything must be perfect when the neighboring *rancheros* arrive for the fiesta in two weeks."

Now Tuhuy understood why Pacheco's men had raided the village. They needed more workers for their upcoming party, and they needed them fast.

Chapter 7 - Vaqueros and Maid Servants

While Tuhuy and the others were being marched to the ranch, Kilik found their trail and followed them. Staying far enough behind so as not to be discovered by the soldiers, he tracked them all the way to *Rancho Caballero*.

He knew he needed to come up with a plan to free his family, and he knew he would need a lot of help. Kilik had heard about another village of runaway Indians that was located further north.

The man in charge of this village, named Diego, was half-Indian and half-Spanish. He had been a trustee at one of the missions and received some military training. That meant he knew how to set up defenses and how to plan attacks. The rancheros, the Mexican government and the soldiers now considered him an outlaw. Kilik decided he needed to find this man and his fortified village.

Riding through the backcountry, he kept away from Mexican towns and close to streams and riverbeds. Indians always set up camps and villages near water. After two days, Kilik came across three Native men fishing in a stream.

"I am called the Falcon," he told the men. "I am looking for Diego. Do you know where I can find him?"

"We do," said one of the men, "But we are forbidden to tell outsiders his location—even you."

"Why do you seek him?" the second man asked.

"To ask him to join forces so I can free my family from *Rancho Caballero*," Kilik replied. "They were taken there against their will."

"Well then, we can take you to Diego as long as you are blindfolded," the third man said. "That way you can't tell anyone how to find him."

Kilik thought this was an excellent arrangement.

"Then blindfold me," he said as he climbed down from his horse. "The sooner the better." One of the men pulled a cloth out of a bag and tied it around Kilik's head, covering his eyes.

"Get back on your horse, and we'll lead you to him," the man said. Kilik did as he was told, and off they went.

Back at *Rancho Caballero*, Tuhuy was learning to use his new job as "the little Indian boss" to help the Native workers. Whenever the foreman's men were watching, he talked to the Indians in a mean tone of voice. He tried to make it sound like he was a tough boss. But when the Mexican ranch workers weren't looking or listening, he gave the Natives words of encouragement. He didn't want them to give up hope.

The workers soon figured out that he was on

their side even though Esteban made him do things he didn't want to do. Things like punishing laborers who made mistakes or didn't work as hard as the foreman thought they should.

Meanwhile the ranch's *vaqueros* weren't too happy about having to train Malik, a twelve-year-old Indian boy, to become one of them.

Sure, the kid could ride a horse. But could he rope and tie a steer, or even a calf? Could he herd cattle from one pasture to another? Probably not. He spoke a little Spanish but didn't have the vocabulary cowboys needed. So, this would make it tougher to work with him.

But Señor Pacheco, the ranch owner, had decided to show off his new, young Indian cowboy. *Rancho Caballero* could boast of having the youngest *vaquero* in the region. So, the experienced *vaqueros* were forced to train the Chumash boy. They had to get him ready in time for the fiesta, because the ranchero wanted Malik to be able to entertain his esteemed guests.

While Malik watched, the old-time vaqueros demonstrated all of the necessary cowboy techniques: rounding up cattle and herding them from one area to another; separating one cow from the rest of the herd; roping and tying a calf; and finally, branding cattle to show which ranch they belonged to.

And they taught the boy all the Spanish words for these activities. For example, rounding up the cattle was called a *rodeo*. This usually happened once a year when it was time to slaughter and butcher the cattle. Raising cattle to be slaughtered was the main activity of the ranch. This was because these animals provided many products humans used and wanted: meat, bones, hides, tallow, hooves and horns.

The hardest thing Malik had to learn was creating and controlling the lasso. Once he mastered that, though, everything else came easy.

The boy had the same ability as his father to quickly learn physical skills and master them. The *vaqueros* were surprised and pleased when the boy was able to perform most of the tasks well within just a few days.

They proudly presented Malik to Señor Pacheco for a demonstration the following day at the corral located near the main house. The ranch owner sat astride his own horse at the fence line to watch. A young steer ready for branding was being held in a small pen attached to one corner of the corral.

Seated on his own horse, Malik waited near the fence on the opposite end of the corral. When he was ready, the boy nodded his head, and the steer was slapped on the rump. The beast let out an angry yelp as his pen was opened.

The steer charged into the corral like he was ready to do battle with whoever had slapped him. Malik nudged his horse into action, and it charged towards the steer. Twirling the lasso over his head, he let the rope fly just as the steer came into range.

Quickly pulling back on the rope, the loop closed tightly around the steer's horns. Malik made a clicking noise with his mouth, and, as trained, his horse started backing up. This tightened the rope as the steer resisted its pull.

At that moment another *vaquero* who had been sitting on the top fence railing ran over and tackled the steer by the horns, pulling him to the ground. Meanwhile, Malik jumped down from his horse and ran to another corner of the corral where a small fire burned.

Quickly putting on a pair of gloves, the boy picked up a branding iron that had been heating in the fire. The ranch's brand consisted of a letter R and a letter C that had been attached together like this: ^{R}C.

While two vaqueros held the steer down, Malik pushed the red-hot iron into the flesh of the animal's upper rear side. The beast screamed and jerked, but the cowboys held fast. After a moment, Malik lifted the branding iron off the animal and looked at the burnt mark left behind. Satisfied with the results, he dropped the branding iron into a nearby bucket of water. A hiss and a cloud of steam were released from the bucket, and the job was done.

"Bravo! Bravo!" Señor Pacheco shouted from atop his horse.

Seeing that the ranchero was pleased with the demonstration, all the *vaqueros* shouted, "Bravo! Bravo!" with great sighs of relief.

No one was more pleased than Malik. A smile spread across his face. Life on this ranch isn't so bad, he thought.

But he wished his father was there to see his accomplishment. Then the boy remembered that Kilik hated everything about these people and the things they had done to his own people.

All his life Malik had heard stories of the horrors of life in the missions. That night, the boy talked to his uncle about his conflicted thoughts.

"I am getting good at being a *vaquero*, and I am proud of that," he told Tuhuy. "But I know you and father, and your own fathers, had to fight for survival against these people. I don't think father would want me to do this work."

"All your father and I have ever wanted for our children is to be healthy and happy," Tuhuy replied. "And it's hard to do either one of those things in these times. I think your father would want you to decide what's best for you, and then do it."

Those words eased Malik's mind, and so he continued to do his best at being a cowboy.

Alapay had similar concerns with her job in the main house.

She worked closely with the ranch owner's family on a daily basis. She came to know the likes and dislikes of each family member. Señora Pacheco, the *ranchero's* wife, was in charge of all domestic matters within the household. The robust woman could be kind to the servants when she wanted to be. But she could also be a tyrant if servants failed to live up to her high standards.

Andrea's daily chores consisted mostly of tedious, backbreaking tasks. But there were a few bright spots in the routine. Those were the times she got to spend with the ranch owner's twelve-year-old daughter, Magdalena. The girl had been spoiled by her parents, and sometimes threw tantrums when she didn't get her way.

But, somehow, the child showed a glimmer of compassion when any of the household servants was mistreated, especially Alapay.

Although the Pacheco parents firmly believed that Indians were inferior human beings, as did most of the Californios, Magdalena was different. Of course, they were all church-going Catholics, but individuals often took away quite different messages from those weekly sermons and Sunday school classes.

Many heard words of condemnation for anyone that didn't believe the church's teachings or those who weren't of their same racial identity. However, Magdalena tended to hear messages of mercy, peace and forgiveness in those sermons. She heard words of acceptance for <u>all</u> of God's creatures upon the earth. In her mind, that included Indians. So, she and Alapay became <u>almost </u>friends, at least as close to being friends as master and servant could be.

Chapter 8 - The *Ranchero's* Daughter

Kilik was able to convince the Native outlaw, Diego, to take on the task of freeing Tuhuy and the rest of the family from the ranch. But this would require much scouting, planning and preparation.

Together, Kilik and Diego rode to the hills overlooking the *Rancho Caballero's* valley location.

Quietly, the two observed daily activities to learn how many Mexican ranch-hands, guards, *vaqueros* and workers the place had.

Then, drawing a diagram in the dirt, Diego laid out a plan of attack. Kilik was impressed with the man's ability to make such a plan so quickly.

"First, we must return to my village and strengthen our fortifications," Diego said. "If our rescue operation is successful here, Pacheco, his men and several soldiers will follow us all the way home. We want them to follow us, because there we can defeat them."

That sounded perfect to Kilik. "I'm ready when you are," he said, as the men mounted their horses to begin their ride back to Diego's village known as the Hidden Place. As they rode, the two men talked of strategies for improving the village's defenses.

Meanwhile, the day of *Rancho Caballero's* grand fiesta was quickly approaching, so everyone was expected to work harder and longer each day there.

The main house was a buzz of activity. Floors had to be scrubbed, windows washed, linens laundered, cooking pots cleaned and silverware polished. Alapay and her mother hadn't worked this hard since preparation for last year's acorn harvest festival back at the Place of Condors.

Out in the ranch's fields, a few of the *vaqueros* rounded up several head of cattle so they could be slaughtered and butchered. Only the best cuts of beef could be served in the cleanest plates on the finest linens to the Pacheco family's high society *Californio* guests.

Other ranch workers had to muck out the horse stables, mend corral fences, build a viewing stand so guests could watch the rodeo, and carry out as many other commands as Esteban, the foreman, could issue.

Inside the house, Alapay worked side-by-side with Magdalena getting ready for the big event. But day-by-day, the Pacheco girl seemed to be losing energy. Her face started looking pale, and she couldn't hold down any food. But, surprisingly, Magdalena didn't want to bother her parents with her health problem.

"Mother and Father have enough to think about now getting ready for the fiesta," she told Alapay. "They don't need a sick daughter to worry about, too."

"I think your health is more important than some party," her Native friend replied.

"But they might call a nurse who will keep me in my room and not let me attend the fiesta," the girl complained. "I do love a party."

"Whether you tell them or not, you should go to bed and rest," Alapay replied. "I will collect herbal medicines to help you get well."

Magdalena reluctantly agreed and went to lie down in her room. That evening, Alapay approached her father for some medical advice.

"The *ranchero's* daughter is ill, Koko, and I need to collect medicines for her," she said. "Have you seen places where our medicines grow?"

"What are Magdalena's symptoms?" her father asked. "If you remember, you have to know the disease before you can determine the cure."

Alapay described the illness her friend had been experiencing.

"This is a good opportunity for you to put your new healing training to the test," Tuhuy said.

"Remember what I taught you about seeking guidance about a treatment from spirit helpers?"

"I must sit quietly and picture Magdalena and her illness in my mind," the girl said. "Then I address the spirit of the illness and ask why it has settled in her body."

"That's right," Tuhuy said. "Then what?"

"Then I picture the land in my mind and ask the spirits of the plants which ones are willing to help make the illness leave."

"Very good," her father replied. "And be sure to thank the spirits for their help."

He thought about the situation quietly before speaking again. Then he said, "I'm going to let you handle this one on your own. It is time. But you can always call on me if you need help."

Alapay wasn't sure if she was ready to go it on her own. But if her father thought she was ready, then she must be ready.

"But you said our Native medicines sometimes won't work on foreign people," the girl replied. "Why would they work on Magdalena?"

"Because last night I dreamed that you will heal her," her father said.

"Wait. What?" Alapay said in surprise.

"My dream helper came to me and told me it was time to show these foreigners that our traditional ways are not irrelevant," Tuhuy explained. "I asked how would we do this, and he said it could happen through the miracle healing you would perform."

Having been taught to believe in dream helpers and miracles, Alapay said with confidence, "Then I must heal her, and I will begin tomorrow."

Next morning, she went to check on Magdalena and found a group of people around her friend's bed.

The girl's mother, father, aunt, uncle and head of the household servants, Antonia, were watching a doctor exam her. He had been summoned from the nearest town.

Magdalena had gotten worse during the night, and she was even paler than before. The girl looked feverish, and sweat poured out of her, soaking her nightgown.

The sick girl caught a glimpse of her Native friend, known to the Mexican family as Andrea. Magdalena smiled and called out to her.

"Andrea, come sit beside me," she said weakly.

"I forbid it!" Magdalena's mother announced. "That Indian girl is probably the one who made our precious daughter sick."

"Don't worry, Magdalena," Alapay said just as Antonia grabbed her. "The land will heal you."

The head of the household servants escorted the Chumash girl out of the room as Magdalena lashed out at her parents.

"Andrea is my best friend," the girl shouted. "You can't keep her from me."

"Now, now," her mother said in a comforting voice. "We can't have those dirty Indians in here while you are sick. We'll get you a new friend, a civilized friend."

Alapay was quickly whisked out of the house so she didn't hear any more of the conversation. But once outside, she knew what she had to do. Perform a miracle.

She quickly walked to a wooded area not far from the main house. She sat down with her back against a strong, healthy tree.

Closing her eyes, the young healer pictured Magdalena sick in bed. Then she pictured the girl engulfed in a cloud, a cloud of disease.

As the young healer watched and waited, a strange feeling came over her. Her whole body began to vibrate with energy.

Then a man's face formed within the cloud, and the face looked back at Alapay. The girl asked, "Why are you here in my friend's body?"

Within her mind, there came a reply. "The spirit of this land sent me to her. To teach her people that they cannot desecrate your people or the lands of your ancestors any longer without consequences."

"Why not bring illness to the ranch owner instead of his daughter?" Alapay asked.

"For the lesson to have the most impact, the

ranchero must be made to feel that something he holds most dear could be taken from him," the spirit answered.

Alapay let that idea sink in before speaking, and then she said, "Thank you, spirit, for helping me."

As the images continued in the girl's mind, the cause of the sickness was revealed. Then the spirit nodded to her, and the face disappeared as the cloud of illness faded from the vision.

Little did the Native healer know that while she was seeking guidance for healing, the Mexican doctor at Magdalena's bedside was about to begin an ancient European treatment of his own.

Of course, in the 1800s, European and American medical doctors were still not sure what caused many diseases and didn't understand how to cure most of them.

So, they continued to rely on an outdated process called bloodletting.

Their theory was that something in the blood might be making the person sick, so it would be better if that person had less of the sick blood in the body. The procedure required the doctor to cut certain veins open to allow them to bleed. After quantities of blood were removed, the patient often fainted, but really was no closer to being cured.

Magdalena's doctor began the bloodletting. The girl's mother cried loudly as the doctor cut into her daughter, but what else could be done? The Pachecos believed the doctor knew best.

Within a few minutes of bloodletting, Magdalena turned ghostly white and fainted. Her whole body went limp. Señora Pacheco shrieked and ran to her daughter's side. Holding the girl's almost lifeless body, she screamed at the doctor.

"Get out, you ignorant quack. Get out!"

The startled man quickly gathered his medical tools and scurried from the room.

Magdalena's mother rocked to-and-fro as she held her child and moaned in emotional agony.

Meanwhile, out in the woods, Alapay continued her meditative search for guidance. She turned her mind's attention to the landscape around her. She could see the trees and plants clearly in her mental picture.

"Spirit of the land, show me which of your herbs will heal Magdalena," she said out loud. Again, she waited and watched as the strange feeling came over her again.

Alapay began to hear a soft humming coming from the ground. Then three different plants began to glow a bright green color.

The spirits of these plants were showing themselves to her. The girl studied each once closely, memorizing what they looked like.

Then the vibrational feeling, the humming and the image all faded.

Tuhuy's daughter opened her eyes and got up. Walking into the nearby field, she began her search for the three plants she had seen in the vision. She placed several stems of each in the burlap bag she'd brought with her.

"Spirit of the land, I thank you for your wisdom," she said reverently and left the field.

After dark that night, the young healer quietly crept up the stairs to the second floor of the main house. The door to Magdalena's bedroom was closed, but a faint light shone from under it.

And that began the first of three nightly, secret healing visits to Magdalena. By the morning after the third visit, the health of the *ranchero's* daughter was dramatically and miraculously improved.

Chapter 9 - The Bear and the Bull

A couple of days before guests were scheduled to arrive, Malik was told to prepare for a ride into the wilderness. When he asked what they would be doing, Pedro, the head *vaquero*, said only, "You'll see. Be sure to bring an extra length of rope."

So the boy mounted up, tied a second lasso to his saddle horn and rode out with a handful of *vaqueros* on this mystery trip. The men rode deep into the woods in the foothills at the edge of the valley.

After a while, Malik couldn't stand not knowing what they were doing.

"We haven't lost any cattle out here, so what are we doing in the middle of the woods with our lassos?" he blurted out. "What are we hunting for?"

"A nice, big, ferocious bear," Pedro replied.

That answer shocked and confused the boy.

"What?" he said. "What's the point of doing that?"

"Entertainment for our guests, of course!" Pedro exclaimed. "But, how would you know that? You're just an ignorant savage!"

The *vaqueros* all laughed loud and long. This confused Malik even more. He thought they liked him. He thought they were proud of him for learning to be a cowboy so quickly. Pedro saw the puzzled look on the boy's face.

"We only pretended to like you to impress Señor Pacheco," Pedro said in a humorless tone. "You Indians are the scum of the earth and always will be. Now, enough of this jabbering. We have work to do. *Vamonos, vaqueros!*"

Malik knew he had to do his job or he would be punished. So, the boy followed the others deeper into the woods. Soon they came into a clearing where a huge grizzly bear was feeding on a deer carcass that hung from a tree.

"He fell for our trap," Pedro said as they rode quietly toward the bear. "Fan out and circle the beast." Addressing Malik, he said, "That means you, too, Mateo."

The *vaqueros* nudged their horses until all six men were evenly positioned around the bear. The bear, now aware of the intruders, growled at them.

He obviously felt they had come to steal his meal. Then, with a signal from Pedro, each cowboy began twirling his lasso overhead. Malik joined in.

Their well-trained horses slowly stepped toward the bear, closing the circle more tightly around him. The bear began pivoting in a circle where he stood, bellowing at each man in turn.

Finally, another signal came from Pedro, and the *vaqueros* flung their rope hoops toward the five-hundred pound, furry brown beast. Two of the six found their mark, falling around the animal's neck. With a jerk, the two lassos cinched up tight.

The animal immediately began pawing at the ropes, but just as quickly, two more ropes found their way to the bear. One caught him by a front paw while the other looped around his snout.

The angry bear tried charging toward one of the cowboys, but ropes from the opposite direction prevented the move.

"Now we wait him out," Pedro said. "He will grow tired soon, and we'll be able to tie his paws together. Then we can wrap him up in those cowhides we brought."

Malik was baffled by the whole thing. How would this bear become part of the entertainment for the Pacheco family's guests? He decided to wait until they were back at the ranch before asking.

The *vaqueros* returned to *Rancho Caballeros* with much fanfare. All work temporarily came to a halt as the bear was dragged into the horse stable. A specially fortified area had been created to house the bear until the fiesta. As the animals was being placed inside the pen, Malik got up the courage to ask Pedro his question.

"How will the bear be used for entertainment?" the boy said.

"Oh, the bear-and-bull fight is a sight to behold," Pedro replied. "We tie them to each other so neither can escape. The bull charges and gores the bear with his horns. The bear slashes and gouges the bull with his claws. The people watching from the stands go wild, they love it so. It will be the big event on the last day of our fiesta."

Malik was sorry he'd asked. This was the most gruesome thing he'd ever heard of. It was torture for both animals.

Just then an Indian worker screamed from inside the bear's pen. Just as the ropes were untied from the bear, he had lashed out with one of his huge claws.

The Indian staggered out of the pen as blood dripped from deep gashes in his chest.

"Indio tonto!" Pedro muttered as he ran toward the bear's pen.

Stepping over the wounded man, he moved quickly to help the others with the beast. The ranch foreman, Esteban, called for two nearby Indian workers to get the bleeding Indian out of the stable.

Once the beast had been untied and the gate to his pen closed, Esteban ordered everyone back to work. But during the rest of the day and the day after that, Mexican ranch hands, as well as members of the Pacheco family, came to see the bear.

Rather than look at the animal with wonder and awe as Malik did, they teased and taunted the animal.

It bellowed and growled back at the gawkers from inside its cage, which caused great laughter among the onlookers.

Malik watched this circus with growing anger. Bears, though dangerous to humans, were to be respected and honored as brothers, not tied up and taunted for sport.

That was the Chumash way. But what could he do about it? He wasn't yet sure.

That night he had trouble sleeping because of nightmares about the tormented bear. At midnight, he'd had enough and rose quietly from his sleeping mat. Tiptoeing across the dirt floor of his family's shared sleeping quarters, the boy made his way outside.

He paused a few seconds to allow his eyes to adjust to darkness. Fortunately, there was a full moon so he could see well enough to find the horse stables where the bear was caged. When he reached the bear's enclosure, he realized he hadn't thought this all the way through. Would the bear eat him after being freed?

That's when the boy remembered the Chumash Bear Song he'd been taught years ago. Did the bear know this song?

Now was as good a time as any to find out. Softly, Malik began singing. It was more of a whisper at first. The bear stirred restlessly in its cell. Timidly, the boy moved closer and sang a little louder. This seemed to calm the bear.

Next came the tricky part. Malik unlatched the hook that kept the gate to the stall closed. Then he backed away and climbed a set of wooden shelves against the nearest wall.

The bear made no move to escape. He may not have realized that the door to his jail was now open. So Malik climbed back down the shelving and moved quietly towards the bear. Suddenly, the animal decided to test the gate. He pushed on it, and it opened.

There was the boy, just a few feet from the giant animal, with nothing between the two of them.

The boy froze, but again began singing his Bear Song. With that, the bear grunted, almost as if to say "thanks" and sauntered away into the night.

Of course, the bear wasn't concerned about whether or not he made any noise, so he let out a mighty roar. It felt good to be out of that tiny space. This caused Malik to panic.

There he was, standing just outside the bear's empty pen. Everyone would know he allowed their entertainment to escape! This was not good.

Malik quickly found his horse, saddled him and rode out of the stable into the night. He wasn't sure where the bear had headed, but the boy didn't want to find out.

Hearing the roar, Pedro soon came running into the stable carrying a bright torch.

The bear was gone and a quick check revealed that Malik's horse was also gone!

"Imbecile!" Pedro shouted angrily. Running from the stables, he headed to the *vaquero's* bunkhouse. Rousting his men from their sleep, he told them what happened. After angry words and a heated argument, the men agreed to head out to find the bear and the boy at first light the next morning.

Word of the bear's escape at the hands of an Indian worker spread throughout the ranch. Señor Pacheco was furious. Tuhuy was worried. Alapay was fearful. What would they do to her cousin when they found him? It wasn't long before everyone would find out.

Even with the rays of the full moon to light

the way, riding out from the ranch in the middle of the night turned out to be a foolish thing to do.

By mid-morning, Pedro's *vaqueros* came upon an unconscious Malik lying on the ground next to his horse. The animal had broken his leg after jumping over a fallen tree and landing on uneven ground. As a result, Malik was thrown from the horse and had landed on his head.

"*Que tonto eres!*" Pedro called out. "Time to rise and shine!"

The boy's eyes fluttered open, revealing his predicament. Surrounded by *vaqueros*, Malik stood up and attempted to run from them. He hadn't seen the cowboy lurking behind a large boulder. That *vaquero* unleashed a lasso that came down on the boy as if he was a runaway steer. One hard yank on the rope brought Malik back to the ground. The cowboys laughed heartily.

"Get up!" Pedro yelled. "Stand up and walk or I'll drag you all the way back to the ranch."

With a headache and a hurt leg, Malik managed to stand. Pedro pulled on the rope that was tightly cinched around the boy's upper body.

"Vamonos amigos!" Pedro commanded his men, and, with the Indian boy in tow, they headed for the ranch at a slow trot.

That speed made it hard for Malik to keep up. He stumbled, and was dragged a few feet before Pedro halted their progress.

"Señor Pacheco will make an example of you," Pedro said with a sneer as the boy slowly stood up. "The others will see what happens when they defy their masters."

Malik wisely kept his mouth shut and endured the Mexican's insults and taunts all the way back to the ranch. Now he knew how the bear must've felt.

Chapter 10 - The Fiesta

Fiesta time finally arrived, and guests from far and wide began to arrive at the ranch. They came in carriages and on horseback with enough luggage to remain several days. Of course, Indian laborers that had been freshly scrubbed and provided with clean peasant garb had to unload the luggage, park the carriages, and look after the horses.

Servants in the main house were responsible for helping guests get settled in to their rooms, rooms that, in some cases, had just been built and furnished. The first afternoon of the fiesta, they gathered in the central courtyard of the house to enjoy refreshments.

A small group of Native musicians and singers performed songs they'd learned while captive in the missions on instruments provided by the Pacheco family.

Alapay and her mother were part of the army of servants who looked after the guests' needs. But Alapay was having trouble focusing on the tasks she had been assigned to, because she hadn't seen her cousin, Malik, for a couple of days.

In fact, it seemed as though he disappeared about the time the bear escaped. Seeking answers, the girl slipped away from the festivities and found her father.

"Koko, I haven't seen Malik for a couple of days," she said. . "Do you know where he is?"

"I'm sorry, I don't," her father answered. "The foreman has had me so busy, I haven't even had time to think about your cousin. Since joining the *vaqueros*, he's been sleeping in the bunkhouse."

Neither Alapay nor Tuhuy knew what was in store for Malik. Without a bear to thrill his guests with a gory bull-and-bear fight, Señor Pacheco had devised a substitute form of entertainment.

Late in the afternoon, the *ranchero* stood on the second-floor balcony and addressed his guests, who were enjoying sumptuous refreshments in the courtyard.

"Ladies and gentlemen, friends and acquaintances," he began. "I had so wanted to thrill you with a bear-and-bull fight this evening," he continued, "But unfortunately, that is not to be."

A sigh of disappointment spread through the crowd.

"But have no fear," the man continued. "I do have another form of entertainment to offer you. So, if you'll step over to the horse stables, we can begin."

As the crowd made its way toward the stables, Esteban, the foreman, found Tuhuy.

"Mi jefecito Indio," there's a matter you must attend to," the foreman told him. "We have an *Indio* who needs to be punished, and Señor Pacheco requested that you take care of it."

"What has the worker done wrong?" Tuhuy asked as he followed Esteban toward the stables.

"He freed the bear and caused much embarrassment to the *ranchero*," the foreman said as he stopped outside the stable and looked right into Tuhuy's eyes. "The punishment will be forty lashes and three days without food or water."

Tuhuy swallowed hard, because he now knew what had happened to his nephew.

"And the punishment will be performed for all our guests to see!" Esteban said with great delight.

"What?!" Tuhuy had never heard of such a thing. "That is barbaric!"

"We've got to have some form of grand entertainment to replace the bear and the bull," Esteban pointed out. "The young, disobedient cowboy's punishment at the hands of his own uncle is perfect!"

"I'm not going to carry out that punishment," Tuhuy said with determination.

"I thought you might say that," Esteban replied as he snapped his fingers loudly. Two ranch hands emerged from the stable and grabbed Tuhuy's arms.

"Chain him up next to his disobedient nephew!" the foreman ordered. The two men dragged the little Indian boss inside the building. Chained to the back wall inside the bear enclosure was Malik.

"I'm sorry, Uncle," the boy said as Tuhuy was being chained up beside him. "It was a foolish thing to do."

"But it was the right thing to do," his uncle replied. "Your father would be proud."

Just outside the stable, in the corral, Señor Pacheco spoke once again to his guests.

"It seems that our youngest *vaquero*, an Indian boy from a village of mission runaways, didn't approve of the bear-and-bull fight we had planned," the *ranchero* said to the crowd. "So, he freed the bear and allowed it to escape into the night."

The spectators voiced their disappointment.

"Instead of enjoying that exciting event, we'll observe that disobedient Indian and his uncle receiving a well-deserved punishment for this deed."

The gathering crowd of guests moved further into the large stable building to watch the spectacle. Seeing the two Indians chained to the back wall of the stable, the crowd applauded its approval of the substitute entertainment.

"The boy's uncle, the man who used to be our *Jefe Indio*, became part of the entertainment when he refused to carry out the boy's punishment, which was part of his job," Pacheco announced.

Holding a long bullwhip, Esteban moved into position in front of the two Indians, ready to begin the lashings. The crowd of people fell silent with anticipation. With a grin on his face, the foreman raised the whip to cast the first blow.

"Stop!" came the sudden sound of a girl's voice from behind the crowd.

"Stop right this minute!"

Señor Pacheco, the foreman, and every person in the stable turned to see Magdalena Pacheco running toward them.

"Young lady, what is the meaning of this!?" her father called out. "Why aren't you in bed?"

"Because I am no longer sick, Papa," she replied. "Mateo's cousin, Andrea, cured me!"

"That's preposterous," Magdalena's mother exclaimed as she stepped out of the crowd of spectators. "She's nothing but a heathen Indian!"

"Well, that heathen Indian did more to cure me than that quack of a doctor," the girl said as she moved closer to her mother.

"That may or may not be true, young lady, but you must return to your room," her father said sternly. "This is no place for a girl your age."

He moved toward her, intending to grab her arm and remove her from the stable. Dodging his grasp, the girl raced toward Malik and Tuhuy.

"This is inhuman, and I won't allow it," she announced as she planted herself in front of the pair.

"I'm glad he freed the bear before the poor animal was gored to death for your entertainment! If you intend to whip these Indians, then you must first whip me!"

Facing Esteban and his whip, the girl spread her arms wide. The foreman looked to his boss, the *ranchero*, for a clue about what he should do.

"Have your men take her to her room and lock her in!" Pacheco demanded.

Esteban turned toward a group of ranch hands who stood at the edge of the crowd and called out, "Pancho! Cisco! Do as the señor says!"

Two ranch hands emerged from the group and ran toward Magdalena. Just before they grabbed her outstretched arms, she bolted away from them.

"Don't touch me!" the girl shouted as she attempted to fight off the men. However, within a few minutes, the two had her under their control.

"If you do this, I will no longer be your daughter!" Magdalena yelled. "I'd rather live with the Indians than remain a part of this family."

"Ah, Magdalena," her father replied with a smile. "Another one of your tantrums."

Sternly he said to the men who held her, "Make sure she gets to her room and stays there." The two ranch hands nodded and dragged her away.

To Esteban, he said, "You may proceed."

The foreman lifted the whip handle back over his head, and the braided leather thong whizzed through the air. Then he brought the handle swiftly back toward his first target. The end of the device cracked loudly as it tore into Malik's young skin. The boy yelled in agony as blood oozed from the open slit of a wound.

"Be strong, boy," Tuhuy said in a loud whisper just before the whip tore into his own skin. A loud groan sprang from the Chumash man's lips even though he'd tried to hold it in.

The whipping proceeded for several minutes as Esteban alternated his blows between the two chained Indians. As blood flowed freely from the backs of the uncle and nephew, many of the women in the audience turned away from the brutal scene.

One female that did not turn away was Alapay, who had perched herself in the rafters of the building. Unnoticed, she looked down on the ugly spectacle, allowing the sight and sound of each crack of the whip to sear into her mind. She wanted to never forget what took place this day. She wanted it to fuel the hatred she now felt towards these people. She wanted to store up this feeling of gross injustice so that one day she could release her anger and rain fury down upon the intruders.

She hoped that day would come very soon.

Chapter 11 – Free at Last

Kilik and Diego just happened to return to the hill overlooking *Rancho Caballero* on the last day of the fiesta. Hiding and waiting beyond view of the ranch was an army of two hundred of Diego's men. Armed with lances, bows and arrows, as well as a variety of firearms, the warriors were ready to do battle.

The ranch was alive with festive activity, and the numerous carriages parked around the property hinted at the potentially large number of defenders the warriors might face.

"There are too many of them to make an attack today," Diego observed. "We'll have to find a place to camp not far from here and wait until their party is over."

"Tonight, I'll make my way onto the ranch and look for the Natives' quarters," Kilik said. "I need to alert my family to the attack. If they know we're coming, they can help from the inside."

"You must be careful, Kilik," Diego said. "If you're seen by the *ranchero's* men, it could tip them off to our raid. I wouldn't want all our planning and efforts to come to nothing."

"The Falcon has never been detected," Kilik replied confidently.

The two men returned to the others waiting below, and they found an area to camp.

After dark, Kilik sneaked into the ranch. A full moon shone brightly from a cloudless sky. Armed guards walked regular patterns on the grounds, so the warrior watched and waited until the coast was clear.

Because he'd raided other ranches like this one, he recognized the familiar two story main house.

He avoided that building.

Peeking inside a few of the other structures, he finally found where a large number of the Indian workers were living. Taking a big chance, he approached the Native man nearest the door and spoke. He didn't know whether or not the man could keep a secret.

"Do you speak this language?" Kilik asked in Samala Chumash. The man replied in a Native language similar to the Yokuts language spoken at the Place of Condors.

"I speak a little of a Yokuts language," Kilik said. "Can you understand what I'm saying?

"A little of it," the man said. "How is your Spanish?"

Kilik switched to the foreigner's tongue. "I speak it some, but prefer not to use it," he replied.

"I know what you mean, but we are punished here if we use anything but Spanish," the man said. "I am known as Miguel."

"That was the name the padres gave me, too," Kilik said with a chuckle.

He removed a feather from his pouch and gave it to the man. "But this may give you an idea of who I am," he added.

Miguel's eyes widened as he realized who he was talking to.

"You are the great Native outlaw called the Falcon!" he said in a loud whisper. "Your exploits are legendary. What are you doing here?"

"I am looking for members of my family," Kilik said. "My wife Kai-ina, my son Malik, my cousin Tuhuy, his wife Taya, and my cousin's daughter, Alapay."

"You will have to tell me their Spanish names," Miguel said. "That's all we know here."

"Oh, right. My wife is simply known as Woman, *Mujer*. Then there's Rafael, Mateo, Abulón and Andrea."

"Oh, Señor, your family is well-known here," the man said. "They are both brave and foolish I think."

He explained what had been happening the past few days, the freeing of the bear, the whipping of both Tuhuy and Malik, and the healing of Pacheco's daughter.

"Your son and your cousin are being held in well-guarded rooms below the main house," he continued. "The rest are asleep here in this building or the one next door."

"Thank you," Kilik said before slipping away. "I am part of an army of Indians who will be raiding this place in the next couple of days, and we need your help from the inside."

The Falcon explained the plan for freeing the Native laborers.

"But you must only tell those you can trust," he said. "Otherwise, our plan will fail."

"There are a few Indians in here I do not trust," Miguel said. "They would do anything for extra food or a day without work. Not a word to them, I promise."

With a gleam in his eye, the man added, "But I will remember this day and proudly tell my grandchildren of it."

Kilik smiled and moved across the room like a shadow in the dark. He crept quietly in between the sleeping Indians to see if he recognized anyone. Finding none of his family in the first building, he zipped across an open space to the next dormitory.

There he first saw Alapay and then her mother. Cupping his hand over Taya's mouth to keep her from screaming, he whispered her Indian name.

She awoke with a start, eyes opening wide to see who held her mouth closed. Kilik then whispered his own name in her ear, and she relaxed.

"You're finally here," she whispered. "I hope you came to rescue us."

"That's exactly why I'm here," he answered. "With a Native army of two hundred waiting just over the hill."

"When?" Taya asked.

"After all the fiesta guests are gone," he said. "Do you know when that will be?"

"In the morning, they will begin to leave."

"Then we'll make our move at sunset tomorrow," Kilik said. "Pass the word so our family is ready. Can you get word to Malik and Tuhuy in the main house?"

"How did you know about that?" she asked.

"I have my ways," he replied.

Just then, one of the ranch guards peaked in through the doorway of the dormitory. Kilik saw him and again cupped his hand over Taya's mouth. They remained motionless in the darkened space until the man was gone.

"Remember," Kilik whispered. "Be ready tomorrow just before sunset."

Before his cousin's wife could say another word, the Falcon was gone.

The following day, word spread quickly through *Rancho Caballero's* Indian labor force. The Falcon would be raiding the ranch before sunset. Native men begin planning on how they would assist the raid while at the same time protect the women and children.

For herself, Alapay was elated. She had envisioned it taking months or years for the opportunity to avenge her father and cousin's unjust punishment. But here it was, today. Her chance was about to happen.

Malik and Tuhuy, however, were worried about how they could be rescued given that their beaten bodies were watched closely by armed guards.

"Do not worry, Malik," Tuhuy said. "Even though we're in no shape to ride horses or run away, your father will think of a way to get us out of here. I know he will."

By late afternoon, every male Indian worker on the ranch had located a tool he could use as a weapon when the attack came. Several of the Native women and older girls had done the same in spite of attempts by the men to warn them away from the fighting. It seemed that everyone wanted in on the action. Everyone was sick and tired of being treated like cattle. Everyone wanted to help win their freedom.

As Grandfather Sun first touched the peaks of the mountain range in the west, a thundering sound could be heard in the distance. Ranch hands and Indian workers stopped what they were doing to listen.

As the sound grew louder, it became clear that it was coming from the west, from the direction of the setting sun. And the sound wasn't thunder from clouds, but rather the thunder of hooves hitting the ground. The Native workers realized the time had come. The moment of deliverance was at hand.

Foreman Esteban and a few other ranchers near the stables peered toward the sound and squinted in the blinding light of the setting sun. Hearing the noise, Señor Pacheco stepped out on the second-floor balcony of the main house. Looking west, he too squinted at the setting sun, not able to see exactly what was making the thundering noise.

Meanwhile, Native workers quietly rushed to find their chosen tools to use as weapons. Picking up shovels, picks, axes, hammers, and even nails and lengths of chain, they prepared for what was to come.

Silhouetted against the glow of the sun, Diego, the Falcon and two hundred Native warriors finally came into view. They rode on horses or ran on foot, releasing blood-curdling screams meant to strike fear in anyone who heard them.

Finally realizing what was happening, the ranchers scrambled to find their weapons or take cover or do something other than just stand there. Pacheco yelled in panic for his men to rally against the raiding Indian force.

Within moments, Native archers released a barrage of arrows that flew through the air toward the ranchers. Those who hadn't found something to hide behind were hit. Those behind cover returned fire with single-shot pistols and rifles that required reloading after each shot.

That's when Native laborers struck from behind the line of ranchers, hitting them with the tools they'd gathered. At the same time, several Natives ran toward the stairs leading to the second story living quarters of the Pacheco family.

Wielding a long-handled shovel she'd grabbed from the horse stables, Alapay bounded up the stairs ahead of them.

"Do not harm the rancher's daughter!" she shouted as she took up a position in front of the door to Magdalena's room. "She's a friend."

Suddenly, Señor Pacheco stepped out of his room at the other end of the balcony. He raised his pistol to fire at Alapay. As he was about to pull the trigger, an arrow struck him in the arm, forcing him to drop the gun and scream in pain. Who could've shot him?

Holding his arm and looking down from the balcony, he saw the boy known as Mateo, the Native *vaquero* who had released the bear. The boy held the bow that had fired the arrow.

But how could that be? That wretched Indian had been whipped within an inch of his life. Behind the boy stood a Native man that Pacheco didn't recognize. It was Malik's father, the Falcon.

At that moment, Alapay lunged at the *ranchero* with her shovel.

Striking Pacheco in the chest, the young woman warrior pushed the man backwards until he toppled over the balcony railing. That was for the cruel punishments he'd ordered for his cousin and his father, she thought.

The two hundred fifty-pound man fell to the ground below with a loud thud and a quiet moan.

The ranch fell silent as the few remaining ranch men dropped their weapons and raised their hands into the air. All warfare ceased.

"Why have you cowards stopped fighting?" Pacheco bellowed from his fallen position.

His leg was obviously broken, but he refused to give up. He attempted to stand, but immediately fell back to the ground in extreme pain.

"Kill these miserable Indians where they stand!" he added through clenched teeth.

The Falcon walked over to the *ranchero* and, using the lance he carried, poked the man's broken leg. Pacheco screamed with agony.

"Forget it, you miserable excuse for a human being," the Falcon said. "Your days of mistreating these people are over."

He nodded to Diego who stood guard over the ranch hands with a few of the warriors.

"Take these men to the horse stables and tie them up!" Diego ordered, and the warriors marched the captives in that direction.

Malik, who was still weak from his wounds, fainted and fell to the ground. Kilik picked his son up and carried him back to the first floor of the main house. There waited Kilik's cousin, also still suffering from his wounds. Kilik laid his son down beside Tuhuy.

"I always knew you would come to rescue us," Tuhuy said. "I just wish it had been a couple of days sooner."

He laughed at little and then winced with pain.

"It hurts too much to laugh," he mumbled.

"I'll be right back," Kilik said and sprinted out of the building.

In a few moments, he returned with two warriors leading a couple of horses. Tied to the back of each animal were two long wooden poles that dragged on the ground behind them.

Between the poles there had been strapped a platform made of branches and reeds. These were portable beds devised to carry the pair on the journey back to Diego's village. The two lay face down on the beds as healers from Diego's village applied medicinal herbs to their wounds.

Meanwhile, Alapay, known as Andrea to the Pacheco family, spoke to Magdalena in her upstairs room.

"You are welcome to come live with us," she said. "You are my friend and always will be."

"I don't think I would do very well living out in the wild," Magdalena replied. "But thank you for the offer. I might have died if not for your healing powers and care."

The two girls hugged.

"My father is a cruel man, but he _is_ my father," Magdalena said. "I lost all affection for him years ago, but I will stay with mother and help her through this time of recovery. And maybe I can help them change their attitudes toward your people."

"We must leave now," a man's voice called from somewhere outside. Alapay knew it must be her uncle. She stepped over to the balcony railing and looked down at Kilik.

"It's a long journey to our new home," he continued. "We want to get there before Mexican soldiers come to recapture their laborers and burn our village to the ground."

"One more moment," Alapay replied. "I must say my last goodbye."

The girl turned back to her friend, gave her a final hug and turned to leave.

"I will never forget you, my Indian friend, Alapay," Magdalena said as a tear formed in the corners of her eyes.

Surprised to hear that the Mexican girl knew her Chumash name, Alapay stopped in the doorway and turned back.

"And I will never forget you, my Mexican friend, Cupcake," she said with a smile and quickly bounded down the stairs to join her family.

Chapter 12 – The *Ranchero's* Revenge

After the fighting had stopped at *Rancho Caballero*, the Native laborers quickly gathered what few belongings they had. They also wrapped up as much food and as many tools they could carry. After all, they had never been paid for their labor, and this would be their one and only chance to obtain something of value.

Diego's men seized all the horses from the stable so some of the women and children could ride instead of walk back to Diego's fortified village. Alapay took two of the finest horses, one for herself and one for Malik to ride once his wounds healed.

"We must hurry," Kilik called out as the two hundred or so refugee Indian workers gathered with Diego's two hundred or so warriors. "One of the ranch hands probably slipped away to report this attack. Well-armed soldiers will be after us very soon."

Diego sent several of his men on ahead to make sure the village defenses were in place and ready for the impending siege. Everyone else followed as he led the caravan of freed laborers and servants to their new home.

On the journey, Alapay took over the task of treating Malik and Tuhuy's wounds, and she continued the job once they reached the village, the Hidden Place.

It was there that Malik, Tuhuy and Alapay were reunited with Solomol and Yol. After Kilik had connected with Diego, the Chumash warrior returned to the Place of Condors. He brought the last remaining survivors from there to live with him at the Hidden Place.

As it had been when Kilik first found his father and aunt at the abandoned mission, this reunion was also bittersweet. Solomol retold his sad stories about Kilik's mother and Tuhuy's father.

"I knew my father had to be dead," Tuhuy said flatly. "I think I felt it inside when it happened all those years ago. I didn't say anything in hopes that not saying anything about it might make it less true."

He was quiet for another few moments before adding, "His spirit reached out to me more than once since then. I think it was to let me know that we would be together again beyond the Milky Way."

In spite of the bad news, those who had just been freed from the ranch were thankful for being reunited with some of their long lost relatives.

Alapay liked to take walks with her mother around their new village home. The natural setting was even nicer than the Place of Condors. A river of fresh gurgling water ran beside the village, and a steep hill rose behind it, providing protection.

But Alapay was more fascinated by the fortifications Diego and his men had built to protect the Hidden Place from frontal attack.

The village sat behind a grassy, marshy area that would be difficult to cross either on horseback or on foot. Tule reeds grew near the back of the marsh, providing good cover for archers to hide behind.

There was a narrow strip of dry land stretching across the middle of the marsh that soldiers would have to use to get to the village.

The problem for attackers was that this passage way led straight to a row of trenches. The trenches were too wide for horses to jump over, but deep enough for archers to hide in. The archers could pop up when soldiers came near, allowing for close-range shooting.

The final parts of the defenses were sets of tall bushes on either side of the marsh that provided cover for another group of warriors that wielded lances.

"Where did Diego learn to build these defenses?" Alapay asked her uncle.

"The man is half Indian and half Spanish," Kilik replied. "He received military training from soldiers at the mission where he lived for a while. Mission leaders were worried about attacks from other foreign powers so they gave him and a few other Indians this training."

"I'm sure those who trained him never dreamed he'd use that training against them," the girl said. "I'm very glad he's on our side."

The former slaves of *Rancho Caballero* enjoyed two wonderful days of freedom in this peaceful remote location. But on the third day, scouts ran into the village's central plaza to warn of approaching troops. Diego sent out the call for his warriors to take up their positions and prepare for battle.

Having practiced and prepared for weeks, each warrior knew what to do. Several archers hid among the Tule reeds at the back of the marshes. Others hid in the trenches with their bows and quivers of arrows.

A group of warriors with lances ran to the thick brushy area so they could close in on the soldiers from behind once they'd crossed the marsh.

Malik was still recovering from his wounds and couldn't participate in defending the village. But, with a word of approval from Kilik, Alapay was allowed to join the protective forces. She took up her position in the reeds and readied her bow.

Soon a platoon of about 40 soldiers came riding up the trail toward the village. The horses in front of the line stepped into the watery marsh and immediately got stuck. The riders that followed stayed on the dry trail and proceeded forward around the marsh.

When those soldiers reached the line of trenches, archers sprang up and released a first volley of arrows. At the same time, archers stepped from the reeds and fired their arrows.

Alapay picked her target, a soldier near the back of the line, and released her arrow.

A series of "thwack" sounds pierced the air as arrows found their marks. These were followed by a series of screams and yelps of pain from soldiers who had been hit. Several men fell from their horses to the ground or into the swampy marsh.

"It's a trap!" the platoon commandant yelled. "Pull back! Pull back!"

The soldiers that hadn't been shot turned their horses and headed for the line of trees behind them.

That's when the last set of warriors stepped from behind tall bushes at the edge of the marsh. They hurled their lances, striking even more soldiers as they retreated.

Instead of arrows and lances, the warriors now hurled insults at the soldiers, calling them cowards, a bunch of children and worse. When the retreating soldiers didn't return to battle, the insults became cheers of joy.

Diego's defenses had worked!

How happy everyone in the village was to see the mighty, heavily armed, Mexican soldiers turn and run with their tails between their legs!

Diego called everyone in the village to gather in the central plaza.

"Let us enjoy this victory while we can," he told the crowd. "For they will be back very soon with more soldiers and bigger guns."

As most of the women and children celebrated for the next couple of days, Kilik and Diego supervised the repair and expansion of the defenses. Branches, tree trunks and poles were inserted into the ground at the front edges of the trenches. This additional barrier provided more protection for the archers when they stood up to shoot.

With the help of her mother and Malik's mother, Alapay busied herself with intensified healing of her father and cousin. Malik was healing quickly, but Tuhuy's wounds refused to heal. Tuhuy suggested that his daughter build a sweathouse to speed the healing.

Sweathouses were regularly used in traditional Chumash villages for purifying the body and soul. These were round, partially underground structures that were heated by hot rocks piled in the center.

Following Tuhuy's instructions, Kilik and Alapay worked together to build a small sweathouse big enough for one person. First, they dug out a round pit in the ground about six feet across. In the center of the pit, they dug an even deeper small hole that would hold heated rocks when it came time for a healing ceremony.

At the outer edge of the sunken circle, they placed the ends of several support poles. These poles leaned in toward the center where the other ends were lashed together. Looking a little like a tipi, the poles were covered with long grasses and mud except for one area that was left open. This would be the doorway to get in and out of the structure.

Once completed, Tuhuy laid down on a mat on the dirt floor. Rocks that had been heated in a nearby fire were brought in and placed in the central hole.

Quickly the inside of the sweathouse began to get hot. While singing healing songs she'd learned from her father, Alapay placed medicinal herbs on the heated rocks. Pleasantly scented smoke began to fill the room.

Laying on his mat, Tuhuy began to sweat heavily. This was part of the healing process.

As sweat came from the patient's pores, it brought impurities out of the body. At the same time, the medicated smoke entered the patient's body through his lungs, the skin and through the wounds themselves.

After about an hour, Tuhuy passed out. Alapay let him sleep as the rocks cooled down and the smoke drifted away. Her father slept the rest of the day as healing energy coursed through his mind and body.

From that day forward, Kilik's cousin healed quickly. After seven days, his wounds had healed enough for him to return to normal life. It was then he began to reconnect with his cousin.

As Tuhuy sat in front of his Tule reed house separating leaves from the stems of a medicinal herb, Kilik approached.

"That certainly was a dramatic rescue," Tuhuy told his cousin. "Riding in from the west so the setting sun would be shining directly into the *ranchero's* eyes! Good planning!"

"Comes from years of experience," Kilik said.

"Years of experience as the Falcon," Tuhuy replied with a knowing smile.

"You figured that out, huh?" Kilik asked.

"An Indian man named Miguel at the ranch told me the Falcon visited him and would be coming to free us," Tuhuy explained. "When he handed me that hawk feather, an image of your face appeared in my mind. That's when I knew."

"Who else knows my secret identity?" Kilik asked.

"Everyone," came the reply. "Everyone knows we were saved by the famous Falcon."

Kilik didn't say anything for a while.

"When we were kids playing hoop-and-pole at the Place of River Turtles, who could've ever guessed our lives would turn out this way?" he finally asked.

"No one," Tuhuy said. "Our world has been turned upside down, and I'm afraid it will never go back to the way it was, the way of our ancestors. Our children and our children's children may suffer at the hands of these outsiders."

Chapter 13 – The Final Showdown

Two Native runners raced into the village just as
Kilik and Tuhuy finished their discussion.

"More soldiers are coming!" one of the men
shouted. "Twice as many as before."

"The turtle-men have returned!" Tuhuy said.

"Time for the Falcon to get busy," Kilik said
as he jumped up and ran off.

Tuhuy hurried to finish his own task of
preparing medicines that he would use to treat the
wounds of Native warriors after the fight.

Everyone in the Hidden Place had expected it—possibly a final battle, a final showdown. Since soldiers that survived the first battle would've warned others about the swampy marsh and archers hidden in the reeds, Diego and Kilik had devised a Plan B. This plan expected the attack to come from a different direction, not from across the marsh.

As before, each warrior in the village scurried to take his or her place. This time, the fight would include both Alapay and Malik.

"I've been itching to get in this fight," Malik told his cousin, as they took up their positions in the branches of a large oak tree beside the marsh.

"You and I are good together, and this is where we belong," he added. "Fighting side-by-side defending our people."

"You're right," the girl agreed as she nocked an arrow. "You saved me from the rancher's bullet, and I healed your wounds from the rancher's whip."

Just then the distant sound of a twig snapping reached the cousins' ears.

"They're creeping in on foot this time," Malik said in a whisper. He whistled a bird call that alerted other Native archers who waited in other trees nearby. Now he could feel the adrenaline begin to flow in his veins.

What Malik, Alapay and the other warriors didn't know was that one hundred Mexican soldiers came to do battle that day.

They brought with them a cannon as well as several Native fighters who had remained loyal to the church and the ranchers. It was these warriors who crept through the woods now. Alapay was first to recognize that Indians had come to fight against them.

"Why do you betray your own people and fight with the foreigners?" she shouted to the closest man on the ground.

"I want to be on the winning side!" the man shouted back as he stood up and aimed his arrow at her.

But Alapay had already targeted the man, and she let her arrow fly first.

The arrow struck him in the upper body, causing his own arrow to fly harmlessly into a neighboring tree.

He screamed as he fell, which alerted other fighters coming through the woods. A chorus of war cries filled the air and the rest of the attacking Natives stepped from behind trees and bushes.

At that moment, a mighty blast rang out across the marsh, followed by an explosion of splintering wood. Soldiers had set up their cannon in an open field beside the marsh. They fired into the trenches that had been filled with archers during the previous battle. But this time, there were no archers to hit. The cannonball merely shattered the wooden barricades at the front of those empty trenches.

Before the cannon could be repositioned, reloaded, and fired a second time, a contingent of Diego's men charged at the soldiers operating the big gun. Arrows and lances were hurled toward the soldiers who had no cover to hide behind.

Meanwhile, a platoon of soldiers began their attack from the other side of the village. Hiding behind bushes and trees, they fired their muskets into the village. Then, holstering their guns, the men drew their swords in preparation for hand-to-hand combat.

Simultaneously, foot soldiers ran toward the village from all sides. But rows of warriors had fanned out around the outer edge of the village just waiting for the soldiers to come within range. At a cue from Diego, archers and lancers let loose their projectiles. Arrows and lances flew through the air with amazing accuracy, striking down the front line of advancing soldiers.

A second wave of soldiers stormed the village, matched by a second set of warriors that let loose more arrows and lances. Each time, more soldiers than Indians fell to the ground wounded or dead.

"These are no ordinary Indians of the wilderness," the Mexican commandant said to his second-in-command. "I can tell by their defenses and their maneuvers they've received training."

"What are your orders, commandant?" the second asked. "Fight or retreat?"

"We must retreat for now," the commandant said. "But we must never cease to fight these renegades. They must yield to the Mexican army or die."

The second-in-command quickly sounded a bugle that signaled retreat. Aware that they were losing the fight, the soldiers immediately turned and ran. Once again, they headed for the nearest line of trees across the marsh, never to return.

The battlefield fell silent, and the Native warriors listened. All they could hear was the faint sound of men and horses retreating into the distance.

Shouts of joy erupted from the people of the Hidden Place. All their weeks of training and preparation had paid off. All their years of just trying to survive as the original people of the land seemed worth it.

Soon, the women searched the area and located wounded warriors, whom they brought to Tuhuy and Alapay for healing.

Able bodied warriors looked for fellow warriors who hadn't survived the battle. Their bodies were collected and taken to the west side of the village for a traditional Native burial. The people would mourn their fallen loved ones before rejoicing in their victory.

Chapter 14 – An Uncertain Future

For several days, the villagers of the Hidden Place enjoyed the peace and quiet of normal Native village life. But in the back of their minds, there lurked a worry about the future.

After speaking with his father and his cousin quite a while, Kilik decided it was time for the family to not only think about the future, but to talk about it seriously. He called the members of his family together.

Tuhuy, Taya, Alapay, Kai-ina, Malik, Solomol and Yol gathered in front of Kilik's house that evening. He'd placed a circle of large logs around a small fire for the occasion.

"This village is no longer the Hidden Place," he told them. "The Mexican government knows how to find us, and it is just a matter of time before they send more soldiers with bigger weapons to fight us again. Since we refuse to serve them, their goal is to wipe us out."

"The flood gates have been thrown wide open," Solomol added. "The lands of our ancestors are covered with an ocean of strangers. Thirty years ago, when they first came among us, I thought they would be no more than a temporary inconvenience. Now I know different."

"I have listened to what the spirits of our ancestors have to say on this matter," Tuhuy said. "Our survival is what's most important to them. For our people to survive, we must hide away our language, our traditional ways, and even our identities as Indian people. We must bury them underground for safe keeping, and trust that one day, these things may be reborn and brought to life."

"Are the ancestors saying we must be like the intruders?" Alapay asked. "Use their language, their clothing, and their ways of doing things?

"I hate to admit it, but that's exactly what they're saying," Kilik answered as he moved into the center of the circle. "I heard this same advice many years ago from a Yokuts warrior at the Place of Condors, but I ignored it then. We can't ignore it now."

"Otherwise you will continue to be punished just for being Indian," Tuhuy added. "My spirit helpers have seen this. They seek to protect us."

The rest of the family had a hard time accepting these words from Kilik and Tuhuy, who had always been such staunch defenders of traditional Native ways.

"What happened to 'never forget who you are and where you come from?'" Malik asked.

"Those words are as true today as they were when our fathers spoke them to us all those years ago," Kilik replied. "You must repeat them to yourselves every morning when you awake. And tell your children and your children's children the stories of our ancestors, the stories of our people. One day in the future—who knows how long it will be— the Samala Chumash people will once again stand tall and be masters of their own destiny."

Members of the family talked of such things deep into the night, making decisions that would affect them and their descendants for generations to come.

Rays of morning light fell on Malik's skin just after sunrise the next morning. Grandfather Sun had begun another day's journey across the sky, and the Chumash boy awoke as the light touched his face.

He'd been dreaming about a place he'd never seen before. There was a village sitting on a piece of land nestled within a bend in the river. Turtles sunned themselves on the river bank as two Chumash boys played nearby. It seemed like a long time ago, but was also very familiar.

Malik had slept in his grandfather's house the last few nights so the two could get to know each other better. Solomol had never laid eyes on his grandson before they both came to the Hidden Place.

"You were just having a dream, weren't you?" Solomol asked as the boy opened his eyes and blinked a few times. "What was it about?"

Malik described the scene with the village, the river and the turtles.

"That's the village where your father and I grew up," the elder said. "The Place of River Turtles was a beautiful home we lived in before the strangers came."

"Do you think I'll ever get to see it?" Malik asked as he sat up on his sleeping mat.

"You just did," Solomol replied. "Your dream helper was showing it to you."

"Time to get up and get going," Kilik called from outside. "We have a long journey ahead of us."

As always, Kilik was ready to go, ready to take on whatever came his way.

Before putting out the fire and going to bed the night before, the family had agreed to move on to a more remote area.

Rather than stay and face another possible attack from the soldiers, they decided to take their chances further north. They'd heard of an area beyond the missions and beyond the Mexican settlements where Natives from other tribes existed with less conflict and trouble.

At least that's what they'd heard. Maybe it was true. Only time would tell.

Continued in Book Three

Afterward

Life for California Natives wasn't as severe on all the ranches as it was for the Native characters in this book. Some *rancheros* <u>did</u> provide some payment to Indian laborers. Some *rancheros* allowed Native workers to come and go as they pleased.

But, for the most part, *Californios* did not treat California Indians well. Many ranchers treated Native laborers exactly as depicted in this book.

If you ever take a field trip or a family vacation to one the California's many historic *ranchos*, also known as *adobes*, remember that, like the Spanish missions, many of these were in truth places of forced labor, poor conditions, and sometimes outright slavery for California Native peoples.

Ask your teachers, your parents, tour guides and anyone else talking about California history to tell the truth, the truth of how California Indians were treated and what happened to the original inhabitants of these lands.

Bibliography of Research Sources

1. Silliman, Stephen W. <u>Lost Laborers in Colonial California: Native Americans and the Archaeology of Rancho Petaluma.</u> University of Arizona Press, Tucson, 2004.

2. Castillo, Elias. <u>Cross of Thorns: The Enslavement of California's Indians by the Spanish Missions</u>. Craven Street Books, Fresno, 2015.

3. Timbrook, Jan. <u>Chumash Ethnobotany: Plant Knowledge Among the Chumash People of Southern California</u>. Santa Barbara Museum of Natural History, Santa Barbara, 2007.

4. Richard Applegate and the Santa Ynez Chumash Education Committee. <u>Samala-English Dictionary: A Guide to the Samala Language of the Ineseño Chumash People</u>. 2007.

5. John P. Harrington's field notes from Maria Solares, Fernando Librado and other Native California consultants. Available through the J.P. Harrington Database Project located in the Culture Department of the Pechanga Tribe near Temecula, California.

6. Cook, Sherburne F. <u>The Conflict Between the California Indian and White Civilization</u>. University of California Press, 1976.

About the Author

Gary Robinson, a writer and filmmaker, has spent more than thirty years working with American Indian communities to tell the historical and contemporary stories of Native peoples in all forms of media.

His most recent films have focused on revealing the true history of California and that history's impact on the state's indigenous people. **Telling the Truth about California Missions** peels back layers of myths and falsehoods to portray the reality of the padres' treatment of Natives. **Tears of our Ancestors: Healing from Historical Trauma** delves into other historical periods and investigates the very real phenomenon of historical trauma. Both are available on DVD.

His television work has aired on PBS, Turner Broadcasting, FNX and other networks. His non-fiction books, <u>From Warriors to Soldiers</u> and <u>The Language of Victory</u>, have revealed little-known aspects of American Indian service in the U.S. military from the Revolutionary War to modern times.

He is also the author of seven short novels in the *PathFinders* series published by 7th Generation/ Native Voices Books. This unique series of books features Native American teen main characters who go on adventures and rediscover the value of their own tribal identities. (www.NativeVoicesBooks.com)

His children's books include <u>Native American Night Before Christmas</u> and <u>Native American Twelve Days of Christmas</u>, published by Clearlight Books of Santa Fe.

All his books are available on Amazon.com.

He lives in rural central California. More information about the author and how to contact him can be found at www.tribaleyeproductions.com. Like his Facebook page: www.facebook.com/tribaleyepro.

CPSIA information can be obtained
at www.ICGtesting.com
Printed in the USA
LVHW080459260122
709218LV00018BC/1075

9 780980 027280